HOGGS

PRISON JOURNALS

Terol McCullar (T-MAC)

ISBN 978-1-77839-085-2 (paperback)
ISBN 978-1-77839-089-0 (hardcover)
ISBN 978-1-77839-091-3 (eBook)

Printed in the United States of America

For those who survived and who didn't survive
"The Toughest Beat in the State."

TABLE OF CONTENTS

UNINTENDED CONSEQUENCES

The rain fell softly through the sodium lights that surrounded the fence line. The 360-degree view through the windows in the tower allowed Wilson to watch lights flicker through the trees in the distance. Headlights on the cars on the freeway that slid along the institution were their origin. An owl flew through the line of his sight.

Most perimeter towers in the institutions are somewhat circular, about ten feet wide and about forty feet tall and usually located adjacent to the fence line. There is a locked steel-reinforced entrance door at its base. Inside is a narrow spiral stairway leading to a steel-reinforced trap door in the floor of the officer's observation area. The trapdoor can only be unlocked with a key or from the top by the officer. Additionally, there is a spotlight on top of the tower that can be maneuvered by a hand grip hanging from the ceiling attached to the spotlight. Most of the older towers had no air conditioning or heat, although many have been retrofitted.

Wilson walked the ten paces around the interior of the tower, squeezing between the off-centered shelving and toilet in the tower. He was exercising, doing deep knee-bends, when the institutional radio came alive. "Control to all units, it's count time, count time."

He walked around the toilet, reached for the phone, and dialed the number for the family visiting unit below the tower inside the razor wire topped double fence line. A voice affirmed, "Inmate Jones, okay."

The inmate hung up the phone and followed established procedure. He put on some pants, shirt, and shoes and stepped out of the door.

Wilson hung up the phone and, from his thirty-foot vantage point, watched the door of the family visiting unit open and saw a figure exit the unit and approach the gate. Wilson picked up an inmate ID card out of a small wooden box and with his flashlight searched the inmates face as the inmate spoke, "Jones D-94361."

Wilson studied the inmate ID card, leaned out the window, and said, "Okay, Jones."

Jones waved his hand and turned and walked back inside.

Wilson visually searched the perimeter of the tower and fence line. He took a count slip from a folder and filled it out. He picked up the phone and dialed.

"Control," the voice commanded.

Wilson responded, "Wilson, Tower 8. Family visiting count, one."

"Copy, Wilson. Family visiting count, one. Good count."

Wilson hung up and dialed again. A voice on the other end reported, "Krause Tower 5."

Wilson started, "So…what's your new job?"

Krause replied, "I think I have D-wing, third watch, Tuesday, Wednesday for two weeks."

Wilson queried, "Who are you working with?"

"Brown and Holtz," Krause replied.

Wilson thought for a second and stated, "That's not a bad job."

"It's a good unit. It has a solid program. It's a good watch to stay busy on, a 180 from these first-watch towers," Krause related.

"Yeah." Wilson paused for a few seconds. He noticed a vehicle driving along the fence line. "Hold on. I'll call you back. The OP is making her rounds."

On the road below, Sergeant Fish, with the headlights off, drove the Outside Patrol vehicle slowly toward Tower 8, flashed her lights on and off. She saw a flashlight coming from the tower signal three flashes. A voice on her institutional radio slightly distracted her focus. "Control to Watch Commander and all units, count is clear, count is clear at 0437," was the notification.

"Watch Commander copies," was the sole response.

She continued driving slowly along the road adjacent to the perimeter fence, occasionally using her vehicle spotlight or her flashlight to illuminate portions of the perimeter fence, the interior fence, and the three-story cement housing units.

When she got to Tower 1, which is combined with the institutional main entrance, she continued halfway around a one-way circular drive and drove along the edge of a parking lot that flanked several buildings and the institutional snack bar. She followed that road as it curved along the minimum housing complex to an entrance gate, where she stopped. She turned off the vehicle, got out, and locked the vehicle. She walked to a gate, unlocked it, stepped in, and locked it behind her. She scanned the older-style wooden buildings of the complex that housed inmates with low security needs. As she walked up to the office, she saw Officer Jones inside. She opened the door and went in.

Jones said, "Morning, Sarge."

"Good morning, Jones. Everything going okay?"

"All quiet, the way we like it. The count slips are in the basket," Jones stated.

"Thanks," she said as she picked up the papers and examined them. She continued, "They look good." She took a breath. "334 inmates."

"It's good that there weren't more. I can't count higher than 350."

Fish chimed in, "Yeah, you might have to take off your shoes and use your toes, and that smell would be lethal." She waved her hand, feigning unpleasant odors.

Jones shook his head and added, "With all the smells coming from the dorms, no one would notice."

Fish nodded in agreement. "Well, gotta finish my drive. Catch you later."

Jones replied, "Yeah, I have to get ready for chow shortly."

Fish nodded and returned to her vehicle; she secured the complex gate as she left. She drove around the minimum-unit fence line to the back side and stopped. She used her spotlight to illuminate the field and fence along the side of the minimum units until she was satisfied nothing was amiss.

She continued driving slowly between a few single-story wooden office buildings. She illuminated the structures and walkways as she drove by. She eased by several older family homes with an occasional bicycle in the driveway. The houses were built in the '50s and '60s to serve as on-grounds family living quarters for the Warden and executive staff. No longer used for that purpose, they are offered to staff on a lottery basis at drastically reduced rents. Rarely did one become available. At the end of the houses, she made a left along a gravel road and skirted the institutional limits. Traversing a levy road that outlined the field that abutted against the dairy cattle fencing, she looked for anything unusual. She was startled when an owl flew across the windshield of the vehicle.

After making a full trip around the institution, she turned back and passed by the shooting range, cattle pens, and dairy. Finally, she approached the vehicle sally port adjacent to Tower 3. She drove on past the vehicle sally port and stopped at the firehouse that was on the opposite side of the road.

Generally, the institutional firehouse coordinates mutual aid with the community. A firehouse has a Fire Captain and three or four paid state firefighters. The jobs are competitive and few, especially the Captain's position. There is a secure staff sleeping quarters and a complete kitchen and lounge area. Also, there may be seven to twelve inmate-firefighters who live in an unlocked open dorm in the building. The inmate jobs are highly paid positions, one dollar per hour. Inmate applicants are closely scrutinized in the selection process. Staff and inmates train daily and maintain the equipment.

Fish parked in front of the firehouse and went into the office. Firefighter Billings was standing at a desk and saw Fish enter. "How's it going, Sarge?" he greeted.

"So far, so good," was Fish's response."

"Guess you want the count slip," he said as he handed it to her. "Sure do." She took the slip, read it, and said, "Thanks. Nine inmates." She continued, "You on day four?"

"Nope, only day two," he moaned.

"Well, you'll survive. We all have to," she said. "That's the plan. Seven more years," he added.

"That beats my time," she complained. "Okay, later." Fish waved her hand bye, and Billings returned a wave.

She turned around and left the firehouse. She got back in the vehicle and drove slowly through the warehouse-garage parking lot, scanning the buildings. She made a U-turn around to the right side of the vehicle sally port and turned into the road along the fence line. She drove past the perimeter Towers 4, 5, 6, and 7, acknowledging the light signals from each tower.

Making it to the other side of the institution, she stopped at Tower 8 and exited the vehicle. She looked up thirty feet to the glass enclosed structure at the top of the tower and walked up to the solid steel door and waited there.

Wilson had seen Fish approaching and opened a window outward. He picked up a bucket off of a shelf near the window and put a count slip in it. The bucket had a rope attached to its handle and also secured to the wall in the tower. He pushed open the window and lowered the bucket out the window down to Fish. "Here you go, Sarge," he offered.

She secured the bucket and took the paper out. Using her flashlight, she studied the paper. She looked up and spoke to Wilson, "Got it. Thanks."

Wilson nodded and pulled the bucket up back into the tower.

She got back into the vehicle and drove along the fence line to the entrance building. She drove around the one-way circle back to the entrance building and parked out front. Fish exited the vehicle and went through the door of the entrance building and walked around to the inside of the counter to where Officer Silva was standing. "Well, you seem to have found a home here for the past year. I guess you're liking it," Fish stated. "Some COs find the first watch job too boring."

Silva replied, "I see it as a respite from my normally hectic day, being a single mom with an ailing mother to care for."

"I hear that," Fish conceded. "Many second watch staff come through yet?"

"Some culinary cops have already come in, and the last two are coming in as we speak."

Officers Roberts and Miller walked through the entrance building door. Fish greeted the two. "Good morning."

The two responded almost in unison. "Morning, Sarge."

The two set their already opened bags on the counter, and Silva checked their IDs and looked inside their bags for contraband items. Miller reached into his bag and took out some beef jerky. Showing it to Silva, he asked, "Silva, you want some?"

Silva replied, "Thanks, Scott, but I have some left from last night."

"Just checking. Have a lot left from the last of my 'smoking' stent," Miller replied.

In Tower 8 above the sally port, Jinks noticed that the radio traffic was picking up. Chatter from transportation and count scattered the airwaves. Silva popped the button for the exit door, and Roberts and Miller exited into the sally port with Sergeant Fish following behind. After the door closed behind them, Tower 1 Officer Jinx nodded to the three in the sally port and pressed the button for the exit gate, and it slid open.

Roberts noticed Jinks in the tower and called up to him, "Jinks, what are you doing up there?"

"Doing a swap for a three-day. Gonna finish this double with my infirmary job," Jinks explained.

"That's cool. At least that tower is busier than the others," Roberts replied, still walking.

Roberts, Miller, and Fish went through the gate, and it slid closed behind them and continued toward the Administration Building. The Admin Building contains all the offices needed to run the prison. The Warden's, executive, inmate records, and investigative services are among the offices in this edifice.

The trio walked through the main lobby of the Admin building and continued through into a courtyard. They continued on, and as they approached a large steel door, Fish peeled off to the right. She walked over and waited at a window at the back side of central control, the nerve center of this and all prisons. As its namesake suggests, in this office, the staff controls, tracks, and monitors inmate and staff movement throughout the prison and both onand off-grounds locations.

Fish looked into the office and saw Officer Brice standing and looking at a large board with columns of numbers on it. Fish, with count slips in her hand, rested her wrist on the window ledge. She noted the institutional count: 4,124.

Brice noticed Fish and stepped to the window and said, "Good morning, Sarge."

Fish said, "Morning, Brice. Here are the count slips," and handed them to Brice.

Brice checked each slip, looking at each slip and glancing up at the large board to match the numbers. Finally, he seemed satisfied. He said, "Looks good."

He continued, "You got plans for your weekend? Reno?"

Fish laughed. "If I had your money, I'd go, but that ain't happening."

When Roberts and Miller reached the large steel door, they stopped. Miller turned and looked at a camera on the wall above and beside the door. He spoke loudly into a box on the wall. "South door!"

Momentarily, a metallic click unlocked the door, and the two pushed the heavy door open, stepped into a sally port, and closed the door with a decided slam. They walked several steps in the sally port toward a large grill gate and stopped.

They looked up at a camera in the corner of the sally port. "North!" Miller yelled.

Once again, a loud click was heard, and the lock on the gate snapped, and they pushed it open. The two walked in, closed the gate behind them, and continued down the corridor.

Center corridor officer Paul nodded to them as they passed by. Paul walked over to a half desk that was attached to the wall and rested his arm on it as he looked down each of the three corridors. He noticed Sergeant Hill coming out of the watch office grill gate. Sergeant Hill locked the gate and began walking toward Paul. Sergeant Hill paused at a control room window, peeked in, then continued to walk toward Paul. "Don't want to jinx it, but it's been a quiet night so far," Sergeant Hill suggested.

Paul drew his face into a half grimace and said, "Dan, you know better than to say that."

Sergeant Hill smiled and walked toward the break room area across the corner of the corridor. He took a key ring off his belt and unlocked the door, stepped in, and clipped the key ring back on his belt. He saw Officer Wong getting something out of the vending machine and said, "Mornin', Sarge."

Sergeant Hill acknowledged Wong, "What's up, Wong?"

Wong replied, "Same ole shit," and nodded to Sergeant Hill as he walked by, and Wong went out the door into the corridor.

Wong made a right turn around the corner and headed down the West Corridor. He walked by a couple of housing wings and the infirmary. He paused at J-wing and stepped into the sally port and looked into the unit. His eyes searched the nearby officer's station and peered through the bars. He saw an officer at the end of the first tier near one of the four stairways of the unit. He was talking to another officer on the third tier. Wong looked directly above him and through a heavy metal floor grate saw an officer on the control panel. Wong's curiosity seemed satisfied. He stepped back out into the main corridor. He was walking past the West Corridor Officer and nodded to him as he locked the Ad Seg door.

The administrative segregation unit, Ad Seg, is like a *jail* inside the prison. Inmates in there are placed there due to institutional safety and security concerns. Wong started to walk by the West Corridor Officer but stopped when he saw the name on the officer's nameplate: J. Yee. "Yee, you're new, right?" Wong inquired.

Officer Yee put his keys in his belt pouch. He looked at Wong and smiled. He replied, "Yep, got here with the last group."

Wong extended his hand, and Yee shook it. Wong said, "Well, welcome."

"Thanks. I guess you older cops are upset because we are taking your overtime?" Yee stated.

Wong smiled, "Not really. It's part of the cycle of the job."

Yee looked at Wong's nameplate and was puzzled. He was trying to reconcile Wong's name with his decidedly *dark* complexion. Yee, being of Asian ethnicity, carefully worded his query. "Wong? That's your name?" he asked with a slight grimace.

Wong smiled and answered with insensitivity. "You're wondering about my last name."

Yee's face showed a "stink face" for broaching the subject.

Wong leaned in toward Yee, and in a confidential manner, he began his story. "I was born in Japan, of military parents. My given name was Bernardo Alowishus Jeremiah Thomas. In the nursery, the head nurse who was printing the babies' names on security wristbands asked another nurse that spoke very poor English to read my name off of the card in my crib."

Wong changed his voice to a voice used to emulate a Japanese speaking with a broken English-speaking accent. "'Oookay, I read name.'

"She was confused by the four names on my card and said, 'He name ees verrdy wrlong.'

"The nurse wrote down, 'Berry Wong.' So that's how I was given the 'Wong' name," Wong said in matter-of-fact tone and waited for Yee to respond.

Yee had listened intently at the story. He pondered it carefully, and his eyebrows scrunched on his forehead. He realized that he had been suckered.

Wong was grinning. He finally laughed and said, "Naw, my dad is Japanese and met my Puerto Rican mother while she was stationed in Japan."

Wong continued, "I get that question a lot. It's not a problem to address it. I am the subject of a fair amount of ribbing, but I give more than I get."

Yee laughed. "I bet you do."

Wong patted Yee on the shoulder and asked, "We're cool, Yee?" Yee agreed, "Yep, we're cool."

Wong continued his rather long walk through another partially opened grill gate past the inmate canteen area and into the Reception Center. When he got to the East Hall door, he grabbed the keys from his belt, unlocked and opened the door. Just as he stepped in, a very loud buzzer sounded in the corridor. Wong yelled to an Officer inside the unit, "I'm going."

He immediately exited the door, closed it, and locked it. He looked to the direction of the sound of the alarm buzzer and saw a flashing light above the door of the next unit, West Hall. He began to sprint toward that the unit.

The radio speaker on his shirt cracked with urgency. "Control, this is Officer Clark. I have a medical emergency in West Hall, first tier. Inmate down."

The radio responded, "Control to all units, there's an alarm in West Hall. Medical emergency, cease all movement."

It continued, "Break. Watch Commander, you copy?"

"Watch 1 copies," was the response.

As Wong ran to the unit with a flashing blue light above the door, Officer Carter joined him. When Wong got to the door, he grabbed his set of keys and opened it. He and Carter cautiously entered the unit. They saw no one in the near proximity, and Wong unlocked the internal grill gate. Jointly, they quickly scanned the unit and noticed an officer standing about halfway down on the left side of the unit.

As the two approached Unit Officer Clark, she said, "Here, take a look." Clark shined her flashlight into a cell illuminating the inmate as Carter and Wong looked in.

Clark asked, "Only one inmate. You guys ready?"

"You might want to glove up," Clark advised. She already had her gloves on.

They each grabbed gloves from the pouch on their duty belts and put them on. "Okay, now we're ready," Wong said.

She unlocked and slid the door open. The inmate was limp, halfway sitting on the lower bunk and leaning forward. There was a rolled up bedsheet wrapped once around his neck and tied to either side of the pipe supports of the double bunk. The rolled up sheet kept him from falling on his face.

They cautiously approached the inmate. Clark reached out and carefully touched his shoulder and shook him. "Baker, Baker, you okay?"

He was unresponsive.

Clark leaned him upright to take the pressure off of his throat. Officer Carter untied one end of the sheet from the bed post pipe support and unwrapped the sheet from around the inmate's neck.

MTA Franks appeared from behind the group with an AED. Clark said, "Let's move him outside."

Almost in unison, they carried him out onto the tier. Carter checked for a pulse and then breathing while Franks did a visual once over of the body of the inmate. Franks leaned down to check for breathing and said, "His lips are blue, but the guy's still warm. Guess I'll have to earn my pay."

Franks unzipped the AED and placed the pads on Baker and turned it on and began CPR chest compressions. After several cycles, the AED voice stated, "Continue CPR."

The sound of running feet from responding staff echoed from the unit entrance. Wong keyed up his radio and announced, "This is Officer Wong. I need a gurney and a supervisor to West Hall ASAP."

Sergeant Perry was standing behind Wong and said, "Don't have to yell, Wong. I'm here."

Wong looked up and said, "Sorry, Dave. Didn't see you." Perry turned to Clark and asked, "Is this the only emergency?"

Clark nodded affirmative. Sergeant Perry keyed his mic, "Control, Sergeant Perry, Code 4. No further assistance needed."

The radio answered, "Control copies. Break. Control to all radio units, Sergeant Perry reports West Hall is a Code 4. No further assistance is needed. Watch Commander, you copy?"

Watch commander replied, "Watch 1 copy."

Clark asked Sergeant Perry, "You want me to put crime scene tape on the door of the unit or just on the cell door?"

Perry asked, "Clark, what happened?"

"I looked in the window and saw Inmate Baker sitting on the lower bunk, leaning forward with the sheet wrapped around his neck and tied to both ends of the bunk. I banged on the door, called his name, but he didn't respond, so I activated my PAD alarm," Clark reported.

Perry replied, "Let me look for a minute."

He leaned inside the cell door and noticed a magazine open on the floor that had pictures of a seminude woman in it. He leaned back out of the cell and said, "For now, secure the unit. I'm not ISU, but I'm sure just the cell is the crime scene, but I'll let the Watch Commander make that call. ISU will take pictures. Someone get a fresh sheet to put over the guy."

He turned and walked toward the front of the unit, keyed his mic, and said, "Watch 1, Sergeant Perry."

His microphone speaker replied, "Go for Watch 1." Perry continued, "Can you 10-19 West Hall?"

His mic speaker replied, "10-4, en route."

Franks was still performing compressions on Baker and was being spelled by Carter. When the gurney arrived, Baker was placed on it, and the two continued to work on the inmate as they left the area.

The ambulance, followed by chase car, stopped in front of hospital emergency entrance. The back doors opened. An EMT was performing CPR on the inmate while on the gurney. Franks stepped out of the ambulance. Officer Miller and Officer Hassan got out of the chase car, locked it, and went to the back of the ambulance, posting up on either side. Medical staff from the ER reached into the ambulance and pulled out the gurney, expanded the wheels to the ground, and pushed its occupants into the emergency room. The officers followed the action. Within a minute, the group stopped at a section of the ER where medical staff had taken over CPR on Inmate Baker.

Franks, Miller, and Hassan stepped away from the ER section

and took a collective breath. Hassan and Miller quickly noted the personnel in the area looking for any potential threats. Miller spoke, "You got to be tired, Franks. CPR is hard work."

After a couple of breaths Franks replied, "Yeah, but it was a rush, given the circumstances. I was trading off with the EMT. This was only my third time doing CPR since I got out of the army."

"Still, whether he makes it or not, you gotta know you did your best," Hassan said.

"Well, I doubt that he survived, only sporadic response on the EKG, but that's the way it is."

Hassan rested his palm on the butt of the gun on his hip and offered, "Miller and I were talking on the way over trying to determine what Brown was doing. We heard a few comments about this being a case of autoerotic asphyxiation."

Franks added, "I've never seen it before, but I thought I saw a girlie magazine on the floor. I would say that's likely."

Miller shook his head and chimed in, "That's a hellava way to get off."

Hassan added, "You got that, right?"

Franks said, "Guess I'll go wash up," and walked over to a wash basin.

Miller turned to Hassan and said, "I'll call in. Can you hang with the inmate?"

Hassan nodded. Miller walked over to a phone and dialed. When a voice answered, he spoke, "Jeff, it's Miller... Yeah, we're here. Don't know the status, but it doesn't look good."

Miller listened a little longer and said, "10-4. We'll stand by for a few and call you back."

Miller walked back over to Hassan, who was talking to Franks. Miller said, "The Watch Commander said for Hassan and me to sit on the inmate and for you to head back." Miller unhooked the vehicle keys from his belt and jangled them in front of Franks. "And... you have a report to write."

Franks released a breath and said in a sarcastic tone, "Yeah, that's great." He took the keys from Miller. "Later, guys." Franks exited the ER and got in the vehicle and drove away.

Collins was following two inmates up the stairs from the fourth tier then to the fifth tier of Building 1 of the second oldest institution in the state. When the inmates reached the top tier, Collins said, "Next time we should take the elevator."

The inmates smiled and shook their heads. They continued the west side of the unit, made a right, continued down the tier. Collins stopped at the corner of the tier. He stood in front of a large vertical metal box attached to a wall. He retrieved a key group from his belt, unlocked the door on the "bar box," and swung it open.

He watched the inmates as they walked down the tier. The inmates stopped by a door. He reached inside the bar box and maneuvered the antiquated levers that slid a series of bars encased in a metal box above doors of the entire tier. Using the proper alignment, he unlocked the cell door, and it slid open. Collins said, "Here you go, guys."

From halfway down the tier, the inmates replied, "Thanks, CO," as they stepped inside.

Collins pulled another lever, and the door slid closed. He closed and locked the box. He turned and headed over to the stairway and began to walk down. As he moved down the stairs, he absorbed his new environment. On reaching the bottom floor, he noticed a couple of officers talking and went over to them. Mentally noting their name tags, Mays and Phillips, he stated, "I guess working the fifth tier will get me ready for a marathon."

Mays replied, "Not much worse than working the third tier."

For a couple of moments, the officers searched the tiers of the unit. They watched the movement of the last of the inmates come off the tiers and exit the unit to go out to the yard.

When the flow of inmates stopped, the door of the nearby officer's station opened up. Sergeant Tom stepped out and called to Collins, "Hey, rookie." He was motioning for Collins to come over. Collins half smiled and walked over to Tom, who waved his hand for Collins to enter the office. Collins entered and nodded to a couple of other officers standing in the office. Sergeant Tom

inquired, "This your second week?"

Collins replied, "Yep, fresh out of the Academy."

"Well, it seems to me that you're fitting in nicely from what I can see and hear about you," Tom stated.

"Thanks. That means a lot coming from an old salt like you," Collins said, admiring the six service stripes on Tom's sleeve.

Sergeant Tom chuckled and added, "Collins, you play checkers?" Tom pointed to a checkerboard on the table.

Collins sort of shrugged his shoulders and said, "I've played."

Sergeant Tom said, "Good. I've got some new blood. How about if we play a short game?"

Collins was surprised and said, "We shouldn't be playing games at work."

Tom said softly, "Well, I'm the sergeant, and nobody else is going to say anything if we play a quick game, and besides, it gives me a perspective about your personality. It's my rookie indoctrination process."

Tom went over to the checkerboard that was already set up and made his first move. Collins went over to the board and also made a move. After several quick moves by both the players, Collins finally prevailed in a rather easy fashion. Sergeant Tom said, "Well, that tears it. Okay, you win."

Sergeant Tom unbuckled his pants, pulled them down to his boxers. He turned around and put his hands on the table and bent over.

Collins was visibly shocked momentarily. He looked at the other officers and said to Sergeant Tom, "What's this about?"

Sergeant Tom looked over his shoulder at Collins and said, "Well, you won. Go ahead and take it because next time we play and if I win, I'm surely going to take it."

For a long couple of seconds, the silence was unbearable. Collins's jaw was slowly dropping. Finally, the silence was broken by uncontrollable laughter of the officers and Sergeant Tom, who was pulling up his pants as he laughed. Sergeant Tom said, "Collins, you passed the test. Welcome to the unit."

Collins was noticeably relieved but gathered his composure quickly and said, "That's too bad. I was looking forward to getting to know you up close and personal, sergeant."

The others laughed, and Sergeant Tom said, "Yeah, you'll surely fit in."

Outside the door, Officer Mays was listening to the fun and smiled. He walked out to the entrance of the building and stood next to the movable podium in an alcove, where Officer Gray was standing. Mays asked, "You see which way Bishop went?"

Gray replied, "I think he was headed over to 'Blood Alley' or the yard sergeant's office."

"Thanks," Mays replied.

He looked out on the main yard, where several hundred inmates were enjoying pleasant sunshine, and headed toward the end of the building. At one of the tables in the notorious "Blood Alley," three Hispanic inmates sat, and two others were standing, keeping watch on the bleachers near the fence next to the softball diamond, where mostly white inmates were sitting.

On the table lay two blue crumpled-up chambray shirts. A Hispanic inmate walked by the table and stealthily picked up one of the shirts and walked toward the fence near the Officer's building. A moment later, a second Hispanic inmate walked by and carefully picked up the other shirt and walked toward the basketball court by the bleachers. One of the seated inmates, Blanco, spoke to one of the inmates, "Pava, whatcha think? Think it'll happen?"

Pava answered, "Si, something might go down."

The Hispanic inmates with the crumpled shirts in their hands stood, nonchalantly feigning interest in the softball game taking place on the diamond. The two Hispanic inmates standing by the table looked between bleachers and saw the two other inmates with the crumpled shirts in their hands.

An officer came out of the Officer's building and began walking by the inmates with the crumpled shirts and continued past the basketball court and around the softball diamond toward the main buildings. An older white inmate stepped down from the bleachers and started to walk toward an area near the Officer's Building, where the open-air urinals were. As he did, the second Hispanic inmate, with a crumpled shirt nearest the softball diamond, purposefully followed the older white inmate.

One of the Hispanic inmates who had been standing at the table with the three seated Hispanics, walked slowly at an intersecting angle to the older white inmate. He joined the second Hispanic inmate with a crumpled shirt and fell in close behind him.

When the older white inmate got close to the urinal, a younger white inmate walked over to the older white inmate and slowed him down by stepping in front of him with his back to the older white inmate. At that moment, the second Hispanic inmate with the crumpled shirt pinned the older white inmate between him and the younger white inmate and within two seconds struck the older white inmate in the ribs and kidney area several times. The older white inmate moaned and began to bleed.

The inmates involved in the attack split away from the scene in different directions. Another white inmate surreptitiously took the crumpled shirt and its contents from the attacker and walked quickly toward the back side of the building. The older white inmate began to slump to the ground.

Inmates in the area of the attack began to move away from the attack. Within seconds, the yard gunner thirty feet up on the corner of the building, yelled, "Get down! Get down!"

An alarm sounded, and all the inmates on the yard lay down on the ground. Several staff members came out of a sergeant's office, and others came out of the housing unit and rushed to the area of the attack.

The yard gunner began pointing to a Hispanic inmate in "Blood Alley" who had gotten down. Yard staff followed his directions to the suspected attacker. They placed him in restraints, searched him, and put him back on the ground.

Officer Bishop saw a shirt lying on the ground several feet away under an empty table. It appeared to have something red on it. He walked over to it. He put on latex gloves, carefully picked it up, and felt something in it. He opened up the shirt and found a flat piece of metal about three inches long.

Two of the officers were attending to the victim. The radio traffic became active. "Control, we have an inmate down on the main yard near the north end of Building 1."

Control responded, "Control copies."

Sergeant James, who had responded from the sergeant's office, replied, "Control, this is Sergeant James. I have and inmate down. I need medical and a gurney, and show this a Code 4 at the moment."

"Control copies. Watch Commander, do you copy?"

"Watch Commander copies," was the response.

The inmate suspect who had been placed in restraints was stood up by two officers, and they escorted him off of the yard toward the main building. A deluge of staff was pouring onto the yard to assist in controlling the inmates in the yard. Sergeant James motioned toward the staff in an electric medical cart to come to his position. Sergeant James said, "Okay, need to spread out and check the back of the building and around the corner for weapons and anything suspicious or that may have blood on it."

Officer Bishop came over to Sergeant James and showed him the shirt with the piece of metal and said, "Hey, Sarge, I found this on the ground near the victim under a table."

Sergeant James replied, "Good job, Bishop. Hold on to it."

The victim of the attack was moaning and mumbling as he was assisted onto a Stokes litter. The litter was lifted onto the cart. They strapped him down, and he was driven out of the area.

As he was driven past the bleachers area, several of the white inmates were nodding to each other, some smiling, and a comment was heard saying, "Chomo," prison slang for a *child molester*.

The long process of securing the crime scene began. Most of the inmates away from the incident were slowly allowed to get up and go back to their units. About forty inmates who were near the incident remained in the yard. The officers began to ID, search, and strip out each of the inmates, writing down the inmates' information.

Back inside Building 1, Officer Collins was following a group of white inmates up the stairs to the fifth tier. As he got to the fourth tier landing, he heard some moaning sounds above him on the fifth tier. The inmates on the stairway in front of him stopped. He told the inmates in front of him, "Hurry. Get up the stairs quick."

The inmates began to climb the stairs somewhat quickly, with Collins following. When Collins got to where he could see the fifth tier, he told the inmates, "Okay, everybody move away to the right and stop and get down."

The inmates complied.

When he made it to the top of tier, he noticed an inmate lying on the floor of the tier. While keeping the other inmates in his view, he went over to the inmate lying on the tier. The inmate was leaning to his side with his knees pulled up to his chest. Collins pressed his PAD alarm. He told the other inmates on the tier, "Move away from the stairs and get back down."

The inmates complied. Collins visually searched the rest of the tier for inmates and noted there were none. Collins keyed up his mic and said, "Control, I have an emergency fifth tier, Building 1. Inmate down."

The speaker on his mic responded, "Control copies. Break. Control to all units who have an alarm Building 1, fifth tier, inmate down. Break. Watch Commander, you copy?"

"Watch 1 copies."

Keeping his distance from the downed inmate, Collins asked, "You okay?"

The inmate shook his head and grimaced. "Noooo…I've been stuck," he said, holding his stomach.

Collins asked, "What's your name?" The inmate replied, "Ruiz."

Momentarily, what sounded like a herd of cattle was staff coming up the stairs. As they got to the top of the stairs, Sergeant Tom filtered out and said, "Collins, what you got?"

Collins replied, "I heard a moaning noise up here and found Ruiz lying on the tier."

Sergeant Tom asked Ruiz, "Can you move, Ruiz?" Ruiz stretched his body a little and said, "A little."

Sergeant Tom looked around at the staff on the tier and didn't see the officer he was looking for. He keyed his mic and said, "Phillips, you on the first tier?"

Phillips responded, "Yes."

"Bring a Stokes litter up," Sergeant Tom ordered. "10-4," Phillips replied.

Outside on the main yard, the inmates from the previous incident were still being processed. One of the Hispanic inmates who were sitting at the table said quietly, "Hey, Pava, sounds like they got Ruiz for us. That makes them even with us, huh?"

Inmate Pava responded, "Si, por supuesto."

THE BEST-LAID PLANS

Sergeant Marks drove into a parking space and turned the engine off. He stepped out of his car, took off his windbreaker, and put it on the front seat. He closed the car door and opened up the back door. He reached inside and took out his wide leather "duty belt." He held the belt in front of him and wrapped it around his waist and cinched it on. He checked the pouches, clips, and snaps that were attached to the belt. He seemed satisfied with his inspection. He retrieved his lunch container from the car and locked the car. He walked past the lines of cars toward the entrance building and looked around the parking lot.

His gaze took him beyond the two-story buildings of the insti-

tution to the gentle rolling hills that contained a sparse number of trees. As he neared the entrance building, he focused on the three towers that were visible along the perimeter double fence line. The two fences were about twelve feet high and twelve feet apart with razor wire on top of each fence with an electrified fence in between them.

He walked through the double doors and saw Officer Chu at a counter. He went over to the counter and placed his lunch container on the counter and opened it. Officer Chu looked into the container and lightly fingered through its contents then pushed it back to Sergeant

Marks. Chu spoke. "What? Didn't bring nothin' for us minions to munch on?"

Marks picked a baggie of carrots out of his lunch container and held them up. He replied, "You mean these don't appeal to you?"

Chu laughed and said, "I'll pass."

Marks smiled, put the carrots back, and closed the container. He ambled toward a door, and Chu pressed a button, and the door lock clicked. He pushed it open.

Sergeant Marks stepped out of the entrance building into the sally, port and the door snapped closed behind him. The tower officer, thirty feet up and to the side of the entrance building, saw Marks in the sally port. He pressed a button, and the complex entrance gate slid open, and Marks stepped through, and the gate slid closed behind him. Marks passed by several staff members and acknowledged several "Good afternoon, Sergeant" greetings with various replies of his own: "Afternoon" and "How's it going?"

He turned toward the AB-yard complex and continued greeting oncoming staff members. He walked to the AB control complex door and pulled it open. He saw Officer Barker in the wired-glassenclosed control room and walked up to the control room window and sat his lunch on the floor.

He reached for his belt and unclipped a key ring that had several brass key chits on it and proceeded to separate five of them from the key ring. He looked at Barker, who was busy on the phone, and Marks waited until he was done.

When he hung up the phone, Barker stepped up to the window and asked, "Afternoon, Sarge. What you got?"

Marks leaned a little forward and spoke through the narrow opening at the bottom of the glass enclosure, "Alpha Sergeant," and put the five key tags on the counter of the opening of the window.

The officer said, "Gotcha, Sarge," as he picked up the key tags. He walked over toward a wall on the opposite side of the room and replaced various key tags with the key tags Sergeant Marks had given him.

He walked back over to the window handed Marks the key tags and said, "Here are Sergeant Parker's chits."

"Thanks, Barker. You second watch?"

He replied, "Nope. Third."

Marks, somewhat surprised, responded, "You're early!"

He replied, "Not really. Paying back a double."

Marks stated, "Well, it's a good job to work on a double shift." Marks took the chits from Barker and kept them in his hand, turned, and walked toward the exit door. Barker reached behind him, pressed and held a button down to unlock the door until Marks pushed it open. He went through, and the door closed behind him. As he walked toward A-Yard, he peered through the chain-link fence, noticing the activity on the yard.

When he got to the A-Yard entrance gate, he looked up at the corner of the building at the tower officer, who nodded to him and buzzed the gate open. Marks stepped in and closed the gate behind him. He turned to the right and walked along the building past several locked doors stopping at the A-Yard office door. Officer Phillips was standing by the door surveying the yard and spoke to Sergeant Marks. "You ready for a fun afternoon, Sarge?"

Sergeant Marks replied as the he opened the door, "Always ready."

Marks stepped in, walked around the corner, and went into the sergeant's office. Sergeant Parker was seated at the desk. He looked up at Marks and said, "Good afternoon, Todd."

Sergeant Marks put his lunch container down, smiled, and replied, "Yes, it certainly is, Bill."

Parker stood up and handed Marks a group of keys from his belt clip, which Marks took, and clipped the lanyard on his belt clip and put the attached key group in a pouch. Parker removed the rest of the equipment from his belt and placed a radio, OC, cuffs, and baton on the desk. Marks handed Parker his chits and said, "Anything going on?"

"Nope. A quiet Sunday morning. Nothing going on," Parker stated and took his chits.

Officer Allen came into the office, and Marks, looking at Officer Allen, stated, "Allen and I will keep it quiet, right, Allen?"

Allen looked at both the sergeants and said, "That's our plan, Sarge."

Allen searched through several pages located on the desk and wrote on one of the pages. Sergeant Parker reached for the pages that Allen wrote on and said, "Guess I'll sign out," as he wrote on one of the pages.

Parker turned to Marks and asked, "Well, if we're good, then I'll go."

Marks nodded and said, "Have a good day."

Parker turned and left the office. Allen said, "Sarge, I'm S&E 1 today."

"Oh, not working the dorm today?" Marks said.

"Nope. Sunday and Monday I'm S&E relief," Allen informed Marks.

"Guess we're in the same mode since this is my second week of relief in this job," Marks added.

Allen responded, "Well, glad to see you here."

"Seems we have a lot of good staff here," Marks stated.

"Thanks. I think so." Allen looked through the pages on the desk and said, "Looks like I'm the first to sign in and you can be the second."

"Yeah, what would I do without you?" Marks said with a smirk and a smile.

Allen smiled and said, "Okay, guess I'll start my rounds." He turned and left the office.

Marks finished putting on his equipment and sat down and looked over the roster. He signed his name on one of the pages and picked up a daily activity ledger off the desk and opened it. He gathered the information from the pages and closed the book. He took a hanging clipboard off of the wall and thumbed through a few of the pages and then placed it back on the wall.

Marks stepped out of the office and walked across the hall to the lieutenant's office, which was locked and vacant. He looked down the hall and noticed that the office assistant Jan was busy at her desk. He turned and walked toward the entrance door, opened it, stepped outside, and closed the door behind him.

He walked several yards along the wall, stopped, and took in the activity on the yard. A sunny day and a few hundred inmates engaged in various activities. Some were playing handball, basketball, tennis, table games, walking, talking, and some were lined up to buy canteen items.

He stood there for several minutes and watched staff come on duty, go into the unit office, and shortly come out and head toward various positions on the yard. He saw Officer Allen walking toward him from the other end of the yard and eventually came over and stood by Sergeant Marks. Both were surveying the yard. Various staff members came out of different housing units entered the yard office and soon came out and left for the exit gate.

Marks spoke to Allen, "I see Bobbitt is in the dorm gun today. Is she up there yet?"

"Yeah, she always gets there early," Allen advised. "She sure keeps the inmates in check," Marks stated.

"She's been up there for six months and keeps the floor cops aware of potential problems," Allen stated.

"The unit seems to run smoother when she's there," Marks said. "She did a good job for me when she was in Ad Seg."

Allen added, "Yeah, she's a good cop."

Marks checked his watch and said, "Guess I'll check the sign-in sheets and see if anybody's missing."

He turned and walked toward the unit office, opened the door, stepped in, and went into the Sergeant's office. He picked up the sign-in sheets and checked the names. Seemingly satisfied, he put the sheets in a tray on the desk. He stood up and started to exit the office when Sergeant Nguyen appeared. Surprised, Marks spoke, "Hey, Cal, no transportation today?"

Nguyen replied, "Just got back and saw you were on this yard today, and thought I'd hang out here for a bit."

"That's fine with me I'll probably need the company," Marks stated and continued, "Have a seat and take a load off."

"Who's the five-day sergeant here?" Cal asked.

Marks replied, "Sergeant Folks."

"Yeah, that's right. He's had this for a while," Cal said. "Todd, I was wondering, have you have any problems with the Border Brothers in your other jobs?"

"No, I haven't. What's up?" Marks asked.

"Just wondering. Avenal has had a few flare-ups lately. Trying to flex their muscles." Cal added, "Officer Allen would be a better source for this yard."

Marks added, "You wanna ask him? He's my S&E today." Cal nodded. Marks keyed his radio and said, "S&E 1, A-2." Shortly, a reply came. "Go for S&E 1."

Marks replied, "Can you 10-19 sergeants' office?" There was a quick reply. "10-4, en route."

The phone rang on the desk, and Marks answered, "Alpha Sergeant Marks."

"Sergeant, this is Officer Bennett in visiting. Sergeant Folks off today?"

"Yes, I'm Alpha sergeant today, but I think Sergeant Folks is working the main kitchen overtime today," Marks offered.

"That's even better. I got some 411 here in visiting that drugs are coming to your yard," Bennett stated.

Marks took a small notebook out of his shirt pocket and opened it and took notes as he listened. "Okay, let's have it," Marks said.

"Inmate Dobbs, K-58326, A-5, 247 up, left visiting a couple of minutes ago. I have info that he's bringing back drugs to his cell. I contacted ISU, and it'll be about ten minutes before they can get there. I thought you could catch him in the act," Bennett said.

"Okay, we'll try to scoop him up," Marks replied. "Okay, Sarge, the ball's in your court," Bennett said.

Marks hung up the phone and turned to Sergeant Nguyen and spoke. "How about you and I go pick up some drugs in Building 5?"

Cal said, "Sure, count me in."

Marks picked up the phone and dialed. The voice on the other end answered, "Building 5, control, Officer Salvatore."

"This is Sergeant Marks. Has Inmate Dobbs in 247 came back from visiting yet?"

"Yes, Sarge. He's just now going over to the stairs toward his cell," Salvatore replied.

"Okay. Word is he's bringing drugs back. Try not to tip him off, but I need your floor cops to watch him and anyone he contacts. If they can, quietly cuff him up and anyone he contacts. I'll be coming in the south corner door in your unit. When I get there, have your cops meet me, and we'll see what he's got," Marks related.

"10-4, Sarge," Salvatore replied.

Marks stood up and started walking out of the office as he spoke to Sergeant Nguyen, "Did you catch that, Cal?"

Cal replied, "Got your back," as he followed Marks out of the office.

Marks locked the office door, unlocked the unit door, stepped out, and locked the door. As they got outside, Officer Allen was walking toward them. Marks and Nguyen walked quickly toward Building 5, and Marks motioned to Allen to follow. As they hurriedly walked, Marks spoke to Allen, "Might need your backup. We're going over to five building through the corner door and see if we can bust Inmate Dobbs with some drugs he got from visiting."

Officer Allen nodded his head and followed with them.

As they arrived at the corner of Building 5, Sergeant Marks got a key group out of a key pouch on his belt and opened the door. They stepped in the door and walked under the stairwell below Inmate Dobbs's cell. Allen followed them in and locked the outside door behind them.

Marks looked around the floor of the unit and noticed Officer Van Vleck standing in front of the Officer's station and another officer, upstairs above them, inside Inmate Dobbs's cell, 247.

Marks had a surprised look on his face. Marks, with Sergeant Nguyen and Allen following, walked over to Van Vleck and asked, "I guess things went down faster than I thought."

Marks noticed two inmates sitting, handcuffed in the Officer's Station. Marks asked, "Is that Dobbs and his cellie?"

Van Vleck said, "Yes."

"What did you find on them?" Marks asked.

"Nothing yet. Still searching their cell," Van Vleck stated.

"He must have dumped the drugs off somewhere or passed it to someone," Marks surmised.

Van Vleck said, "They haven't contacted anyone since they came in. We cuffed them and put them in our office. They haven't been searched yet."

Marks had an incredulous stare on his face, and his jaw dropped open. He looked at Sergeant Nguyen and shook his head. He looked back at Van Vleck and spoke deliberately, "You mean you put them in your office and didn't search them?"

Van Vleck responded, "Yes. Sergeant Folks came in just before you got here and told me to put them in the office and had Officer Taylor search their cell. Then he left."

"Sergeant Folks didn't have you search them?" Marks asked. "No, he just said to cuff them, put them in the office, and keep

an eye on them," Van Vleck replied.

Sergeant Marks took a slow breath. He turned to Allen and said, "Allen, you and Van Vleck take these inmates over to the shower area and strip them out. When you get done, put them in a holding cell."

Allen nodded his head and said to Van Vleck, "Okay, Ed, let's do it."

The officers went into the office, retrieved the inmates, and escorted them toward the shower area. Marks turned to Sergeant Nguyen and asked, "Well, Cal, where you think the drugs are?"

Sergeant Nguyen smiled, looked into the office, and nodded toward it. Marks nodded in agreement.

The officer in the secured control room on the second floor of the housing unit saw two Investigative Services Unit officers at the outside door. He pressed a button on a panel, and the door slid open. The officers walked in and stopped in the short corridor. The officer looked down into the sally port through a thick glass sectioned off above it and saw that they were clear of the door and pressed another button that closed the door. The officer pressed another button that slid that grill gate open.

ISU Officers Pool and Knox come in the unit. They looked around the floor and saw Sergeant Marks and walked over to him. "Sergeant Marks, what's up?" Officer Knox asked.

Marks replied, "Well, Bennett in visiting called me and said he was informed that Inmate Dobbs had gotten drugs from a visitor. Cal, Allen, and I came over to check it out. When we got here, Taylor was searching their cell and Dobbs and his cellmate were cuffed and sitting in the Officer's station.

"Van Vleck was watching them from outside the office. He told me they hadn't been searched yet. I had my S&E, Allen, and Van Vleck take the inmates to the shower area and strip them out. That's what you've got."

Knox replied, "Yeah, we got the call from visiting about the drugs, but"—Knox glanced over toward the shower area and back toward the office and seemed puzzled.

"Why weren't the inmates searched before they put them in the office?"

Marks replied, "That's something you'll have to ask Sergeant Folks. Apparently, he got wind of the drug bust and got here first."

"Okay, where's Sergeant Folks?" Knox asked.

"I guess he went back to the main kitchen, where he was working overtime," Marks replied. "You might want to search the Officer's Station. Just a suggestion."

While shaking his head, Knox said, "Well, whatever we find in there won't do us any good."

Marks smiled and said, "Well, if you need me, I'll be in my office writing my report."

Knox nodded and turned to his partner Officer Pool and asked, "You want to search the office or the inmates?"

Officer Pool replied, "Doesn't matter much now. This bust is a bust."

Sergeant Marks walked over to Allen and said, "Hey, Allen, ISU is going to take over. When they do, I guess you can finish your S&E stuff, and when you get a chance, write a report on any part you played in this." Marks waved his hands in exasperation.

"Okay, Sergeant," Allen replied.

Marks and Cal walked over to the sally port gate and looked up at Control Officer Salvatore and said loudly, "Going out!"

The gate slid open, and Marks and Cal stepped into the sally port. The gate slid behind them, and the exit door in front of them slid open. They walked through the door, and Marks yelled, "Clear!" and the door slid closed behind them.

Marks and Nguyen strolled across the yard to the unit office, unlocked the door, stepped in, locked it behind them, unlocked the sergeant's office door, and went in. Marks and Cal sat down at the desk. They glanced at each other, both with knowing smirks on their faces. "Well," Marks started, "I guess Folks wanted the credit for the bust."

Cal paused momentarily, shook his head, and spoke with a chuckle, "I'm sure when the lieutenant reads the package, she'll have some questions to ask him."

Marks nodded while logging on to the computer and said, "I'll just tell it like it happened. Gonna be a waste of time. No case here."

Cal added. "Yeah, and ISU's gonna be pissed."

The phone rang, and Marks answered, "Sergeant Marks, A-Yard."

The voice on the other end replied, "Yeah, Sarge, Knocks here."

Marks replied, "What's up, Knocks? Uh, hold on, can I put you on speaker? Sergeant Nguyen is here too."

"Sure," Knocks said.

Marks pressed the speaker button. "Okay, go ahead, Knocks.

But first, let me guess: you found the drugs."

Knocks replied, "Yep, and you know where too." Marks said, "I can only guess."

Cal excitedly interrupted the conversation, holding a hand up and hopping up and down in his chair, "Ooh, ooh, can I guess?"

Marks laughed and said, "Cal wants a crack at the guess." Knocks replied, "Well...okay, but only one guess."

"In the officer's station," Cal said emphatically.

Knocks laughed and said, "Ding, ding. You win. Big surprise, huh? Anyway, I look forward to your reports."

"We're sure you are. Thanks, Knocks, for the follow-up," Marks quipped.

Knocks sang his reply, "That's what friends are for."

Marks laughed and said, "Later, Bro." He disconnected the call.

Marks started typing his report and asked Cal, "You want to do yours after mine?"

Cal replied, "Sure. I can write that I didn't see or do anything. End of report." He added, "I wonder how the officers are going to explain why they found drugs in their office."

They laughed.

LIE TO STAY ALIVE

Officer Banks stopped at the corner of the corridors in the Reception Center and sat his lunch container he had been carrying on the floor. He reached to his duty belt and unhooked a small ring of chits and pealed six tags off the ring and snapped the ring back on his duty belt. He waited at the RC control window for Officer Wilson to finish his tasks at hand. Banks looked down the corridors, noticing various staff moving about. Wilson stepped up to the window and asked Banks, "What you got?"

Banks put the six chits on the window ledge and replied, "S&E 1, an East Hall dining door key, and a mic with the radio. That's six dollars."

Wilson scooped up the chits and wheeled around and retrieved the various equipment for boards and racks and put the chits on related hooks and came back with the items requested and set them on the ledge. Banks nodded and said, "Thanks, bud." He grabbed the equipment and stepped aside.

He clipped the lanyard of one of the key groups on his duty belt and placed the attached key group in a belt pouch. He clipped the other key on a separate belt clip. He took the baton, opened it, closed it, and placed it in the holder on his belt. He retrieved a key ring from his belt that had a staff key and handcuff key on it. He picked up the handcuffs, ratcheted them around. He locked the each cuff with the cuff key and tried to ratchet them around to ensure they didn't ratchet. He unlocked the cuffs, ratcheted them around, and put them in his cuff case.

Next, he picked up the canister of OC pepper spray, shook it, and put it in a holder on his belt. Lastly, he picked up the radio, checked the settings, put it in the holder on his belt, and clipped the remote mic onto his shoulder epaulet, turned it on, and keyed it up. He heard the static coming from the radio in the RC control room. He picked up his lunch container and walked toward the sergeant's office.

Reception Center (RC) Sergeant Perry's sleeve was emblazoned with eight service stripes for the twenty-four plus years on the job. He was respected by staff and inmates alike. He was sitting at his desk in the sergeant's office. Banks, with one stripe, stepped into his office. He told Perry, "I have East Hall dining. I'll go see if they are ready to feed chow."

Perry nodded, stood up, followed Banks out the door, and locked it. Banks rounded the corner and eased into the East Hall housing unit entrance. He unlocked the gate to the Officer's Station and put his lunch down. He stepped out locked that gate and stepped to the sally port grill gate, unlocked and opened it, stepped into the housing unit, and locked the grill gate behind him.

He looked down the tier and saw Officer Riggs on the west side of the second tier. Banks turned and looked up behind him to the second floor behind the bars and saw Officer Rogers seated at the control panel. Through the bank of wire encased windows, he noticed that Officer Bautista was in the dining hall sitting at one of the tables waiting for chow to start. He walked over to the dining hall door, unlocked it, and opened it all the way. He clipped the key back onto his belt. Banks waved to Bautista and walked partway into the dining hall and called out, "Foster, you ready?"

Dining Hall CO Foster stepped out from the behind the steam line and replied, "Yeah, send 'em."

Banks, seeing Foster, nodded and went back out the opened door and posted up outside the door. Banks reached to the glove pouch on his duty belt and took out a pair of latex gloves and put them on. Standing in the corridor, Sergeant Perry keyed his mic and spoke. "East Hall, West Hall, are you ready to do this?"

Banks responded, "10-4, East Hall is ready."

Another report over the radio stated, "West Hall is up and ready."

Perry again keyed his mic, "West Hall and East Hall, send your patrons to chow."

Banks yelled up behind him to the officer on the control panel, "Rogers, bust 'em loose."

Rogers yelled out, "Tier 3, East side, Chow. Step out."

The third tier doors slid open, and the inmates sporadically made their way off the tier and down the stairs to the unit floor ambling to chow, all of this under the watchful eyes of Unit Officer Riggs on the opposite third tier west side and Rodgers on the panel up in front of the unit above Banks.

The inmates shuffled down the stairs in their state-supplied orange jumpsuits and slippers. They continued toward Banks and eventually into the dining hall. Banks by habit noticed the demeanor and features of the passersby. Occasionally, Banks would remind an inmate to pull up their pants and/or tuck their shirt in.

Randomly, Banks would back away from the line and point his hand to an inmate and then, in a universal motion, to the ground in front of him to direct the inmate to submit to a pat down. Banks would usually greet the inmate with a nod, "Good morning," or "How's it going?"

Occasionally, an inmate might be new to the process and have to be directed specifically what to do, as was the case with one inmate. He directed the inmate. "Step over here, guy."

The inmate came over to Banks.

"Can you stand here?" Banks pointed to the floor in front of him.

The inmate did as requested.

"Hand me your ID."

The inmate gave him his ID. Banks took it, read it, put it his shirt pocket, and said, "Mr. Jackson, can you turn around and face away and raise their arms out to your sides?"

He complied. The inmate's hand had a pack of hot sauce and a molded state-supplied spoon in his hand. Banks retrieved them, inspect them, and put them back in the inmate's hand. Banks said, "Okay, Jackson, I'm gonna pat you down. Don't move, okay?"

Jackson nodded. Keeping aware of the other inmates, Banks went through the search process, starting at the collar to the shoulders, under the arms, sides, back, the chest, stomach, waist, top of the groin, each leg, then up between the legs, and using the back of his hand, pushing up gently to the scrotum. When he was finished, he gave the inmate his ID back and said, "Thanks. Enjoy your meal." After that section of the tier emptied, Rogers called out, "Tier 2, east side, chow. Step out."

The same process was implemented for the second tier. When the second tier was empty, Riggs walked around the walkway to the east side of the third tier and looked into each cell and slid the door closed and then down the stairs to the second tier and closed those doors.

On entering the dining hall, the inmates would funnel through a railed walkway to the steam line, where they would pick up a prepared tray of food from an opening and continue around to some large canisters containing the liquid offering of the day. Coffee, juice, water, or a carton of state-processed milk was the normal fare.

After the stream of all the patrons entered the dining hall, Banks closed the door and locked it from the outside. After about twenty minutes, Banks noticed that most all the inmates were sitting, waiting.

Bautista was standing next to the back wall watching the inmates. Banks saw Riggs back on the west side of the tiers and held a thumbs-up. Riggs gave a thumbs-up signal. Banks called up to Rogers on the panel, "Rogers, you ready?"

Rogers replied, "Yep."

Banks unlocked and opened the dining hall door and gestured to Bautista in a signal to see if he was ready to release the inmate to go back to their cells. Bautista nodded and went table to table and motioned to the four seated at each table that it was time to go. The inmates complied and, taking their trays and beverage containers with them, walked along the wall stopping to dump out any excess food into a trash container and stack their trays on a cart and put their cups in a bin.

Banks stood outside the door and watched each inmate file out of the dining hall and up the stairs. As the inmates got to the door of their assigned cell, they stood in front of it. When the tier was full, Riggs yelled out to Rogers, "Open third tier."

When the doors opened, the inmates stepped inside their cell. When the tier was clear, Riggs yelled to Rogers. "Close 'em." The doors closed.

This processed continued for each tier until the last of the three tiers was released to come to the dining hall. The dreaded sound of a buzzer was faintly heard and was followed by an announcement on the radio: "We have an alarm in West Hall. Control, you copy?"

"Control copies. Break! Control to all units, there is an alarm in West Hall. RC Sergeant, you copy?

Sergeant Perry keyed his mic while he responded to West Hall, "RC Sergeant copies. En route."

Banks rushed the remaining inmates into the dining hall, unclipped the dining hall key from his belt, and in doing so, tore his glove. He locked the door, clipped the key back to his belt, and watched the inmates from outside.

Riggs saw that the unit was secure and began running toward Banks and the unit exit. Banks saw him coming and unlocked the sally port grill gate to let Riggs out. As he exited, Banks locked the gate and went back to the dining hall door and continued watching the inmates. He listened intently to the radio for more reports about the incident.

Waiting for radio interaction when an incident was happening serves as a time for introspection. Wondering about the dangers involved in quelling even a minor incident is pondered. A simple body search can turn violent. Just responding to an emergency is hazardous, not to mention a full blown building or yard riot that can result in deadly consequences for inmates and staff.

After several minutes, the radio finally crackled. "Control, this is RC Sergeant Perry. I have a Code 4. No further response is needed. Break. Control, I have an escort to mainline infirmary turn on the light."

"Control copies."

The radio traffic continued. "Break…Watch Commander, this is central control. RC Sergeant reports a Code 4. Request to resume."

"This is the Watch Commander, 10-4. Resume normal."

"Control copies. Break…control to all units, resume normal movement."

Banks speculated what could have happened in the building next to him. Momentarily, Riggs came back into the unit. Banks inquired. "What's up?"

Riggs replied, "Seems the staff saw an inmate had some bruises on his face when he came to chow, so they froze the movement and took him aside. His cellie admitted he touched him up, so they gaffed him up and put them in a holding cage. The vic was taken to the infirmary to get checked out."

Banks shook his head and said, "No staff hurt?"

"Nope," was Riggs's reply.

Banks, in relief, said, "Good."

Riggs walked down the tier to get ready for the inmates to go back to their cells. Banks went over to the dining hall door and saw Bautista waiting with the inmates, who were more than finished eating. Banks opened the door, and Bautista began his exit routine.

Bautista ushered the last of the group of inmates out of the dining hall. Banks went over to Foster and Bautista. Bautista asked, "What was the alarm about?"

"Apparently, an inmate was assaulted in his cell last night by his cellie, and they noticed bruises on the inmate when he came out for chow and pulled him out of line. His cellie owned up to the assault."

Bautista said, "Just another day at the funny farm."

Foster turned and walked over and stepped behind the steam line. Bautista called out to Foster. "Okay, Foster, see you on the yard."

Foster called back, "Yep, see you there."

Banks added, "Hey, Foster, good job with the chow, homie."

Foster smiled.

Banks went out of the dining hall and locked the door. He clipped the key back on his belt and retrieved the other key group from his belt. He walked over to the grill gate, unlocked it, stepped through, and locked it behind him. He turned to his right and unlocked another gate and went in.

In this area was a staff bathroom and some storage and floor cleaning equipment. He opened the door to the bathroom, took off the latex gloves, discolored from the body searches and key residue, and tossed them into a nearby trash can.

After he washed his hands, he went back through the gate, locked it, and clipped the key group onto his belt. He stepped out into the corridor and walked a few steps ahead and stood at the RC control window. He unclipped the Dining Hall door key from his belt and handed it to Wilson, who anticipated Banks's intent and had his key chit waiting to exchange it for the key and handed it to Banks. "Thanks," Banks said.

Wilson smiled and said, "You got it"

Banks reached for his key ring with the chits and cuff key on it to put the single chit back on it. His hand failed to find the familiar key ring on its normal key clip. He looked down and didn't see it on his belt. He felt for the ring again on other parts of his belt and took the other key group out of its pouch to see if the missing ring was accidentally attached somehow to it. No dice.

Banks took a slow breath of anxiety. He looked around on the ground to see if the errant key ring was there. Again, there was no sign of it. Quickly, he checked his pockets. Not there.

He turned back to Wilson and asked him with urgency, "Hey, buddy, did you happen to see a key ring of chits on the counter? I can't find mine. The last time I used it was when I got my keys this morning."

Wilson shook his head with concern. "No, partner…didn't see it this morning when you got your equipment and not just now either."

Banks's face showed anxiety. "Oh, crap. It has my chits, staff key, and a cuff key on it."

Wilson returned concern. "Wow! That's messed up. Can't let an inmate get hold of that key ring. The staff key can get them into several sensitive areas, not to mention the reports and the cost of rekeying all the staff locks and replacing the staff keys of all the employees. Losing a cuff is in itself really dangerous. I feel for you, brother."

Banks, still searching his person, said, "I'm gonna check back in East Hall."

Wilson replied, "Yeah, good idea."

Banks put the single chit in his pants pocket, wheeled around, and retraced his steps back to East Hall through the gates and to the dining hall door. The search was fruitless. He started back to check the Officer's Station and bathroom when the radio summoned his attention: "RC S&E Banks, 10-19, RC sergeant's office."

That request was hopefully a good sign. Banks responded, "10-4."

He hurried through the doors, again unlocking and locking them. He turned the corner in the corridor and saw Sergeant Perry at his desk and opened the door and went it. Banks was half holding his breath and pleaded, "Perry, tell me you found my key ring."

Perry looked up at Banks and said, "What key ring?"

Banks's pain was visible. "Ugh, I lost my key chit ring with my staff key and cuff key on it."

Perry's eyebrows darkened, and a slight scowl wrinkled his face. He took a deep breath and paused pensively before he spoke. "You know"—he paused again—"I know you're a straight-up cop, and you don't duck responsibility. I was going to let you squirm but..." He held up the missing key ring. "Riggs found this by the dining room door."

Banks with a noticeable sigh, said, "Thanks, Sarge." He took the key ring and inspected its contents, took the single chit out of his pants pocket, put it back on the key ring, and clipped the ring securely on his key holder. "I went back to there to look for them when I turned the dining hall key." He shook his head and continued to explain, "I retraced my steps and came up empty. The blood seemed to drain from my head when I noticed the ring missing, knowing all the problems that represented."

Perry smiled and said, "I've known your good work and dedication for a while, and we've all been in these scary situations."

Banks's mind was searching. "I think I know what happened. When the alarm went off, I got the door key off my belt and caught my glove on it. That might have caught the other key ring."

Perry offered, "Well, now you owe your ass to Riggs."

"I sure do." He paused. "You need a memo or anything from me. I'll sign any write up you need."

Perry shook his head. "No, nada. Like I said, we've all been there. Just take this as a learning experience."

Banks sighed. "Thanks, Sarge. I'll go find Riggs and see what kind of new car he wants."

Perry laughed. "Okay. But after that, you need to pick up Inmate Sanders in the infirmary and bring him back. I want to talk to him. He's the assault victim from West Hall this morning."

"Copy that, Sarge."

Banks started to turn when Perry noticed his uniform sleeve.

Perry said, "Wait a minute."

Banks stopped. Perry pointed at Banks's uniform and asked, "What's wrong with your uniform?"

Banks glance down at his uniform and noticed no irregularity and said, "Just a uniform."

Perry leaned back in his chair and continued, "How long you been on the job?"

Banks replied slowly, "Going on six years."

Perry added, "I thought so. You know it's out of compliance?" Banks was perplexed.

"Look at your left sleeve."

Banks looked but didn't see anything amiss.

"You only have one hash mark. You know you can put another service stripe on six months before your anniversary date."

Banks smiled, snapped to attention, saluted, and said emphatically, "Yes, Sergeant! Will that be all, Sergeant?"

Perry laughed and waved Banks out.

Banks left the office and went directly to East Hall and found Riggs in the Officer's Station. He went over to Riggs and shook his hand. "Hey, Bro, you saved my ass."

Riggs said, "When I saw the key ring and saw it was yours, I tried to catch up to you but didn't see you."

Banks explained, "I stopped off in the bathroom to wash my hands. That must have been how you missed me."

"Yeah, I thought you disappeared too quickly."

"Anyway, you saved me." He grabbed his hand and brought him close in a hug and back pat.

"No problem, Bro. I got your back," Riggs exalted. Banks added, "You need a new car or boat?"

Riggs smiled. "Now that you mention it..." He stopped and laughed. He pushed Banks away and said, "Just quit dropping your shit in my unit."

Banks said, "Thanks again." He took a deep breath. "Well, I gotta go pick up this morning's vic at the infirmary."

Riggs said, "Then get your butt moving."

Banks left the unit and headed down the corridor to the infirmary.

As Banks arrived at the infirmary entrance, CO Kelly was lining up some inmates dressed in orange jumpsuits for escort. Banks asked, "These guys going to RC?"

Kelly said, "Yeah. Waiting for the bus to pick them up."

"Well, I can run them down. Just gotta pick up the West Hall assault victim and take him back."

Kelly said, "That's cool. I think he's in the room right here," pointing to the room just inside the door and handing Banks an inmate ID.

Banks said, "I'll get him."

He looked into the room through the wire glass window and saw an inmate wearing orange, sitting on a chair and RN Walker at a counter. He stepped over to the door and opened it. He nodded to Walker and, looking at the ID, asked, "What's your name and number?"

"John Sanders. My number is DD something. Haven't memorized it yet." He was obviously very nervous.

Banks shook his head and verified the picture and that the number started with DD.

"Where do you live?"

"Tulare."

Banks's eyebrows raised. He noticed Walker chuckling. "No, I mean what unit and cell are you assigned to?"

"West Hall, somewhere on the second tier," he replied. Banks shrugged and shook his head. "Can you walk?"

"Yes, sir, I can walk," he stated.

Banks asked Walker, "You have a 7219 for this guy?"

Walker said, "Yeah, he's ready to rock 'n' roll," handing the medical evaluation report to Banks, who folded it and put it inside his protective vest.

He turned to Sanders. "You gonna be okay to walk with these other inmates down to RC?" Banks asked, pointing to the inmates outside the door.

"I guess. Why?"

Banks pressed further. "I mean, do you know any of them from your housing unit?"

"I don't think so."

Banks asked, "You gonna give me any problem on the way, or do I have to put you in cuffs?"

"No, sir, I'll do what you tell me."

Banks took a deep breath and said, "Okay, let's go."

Banks stepped back away from the door into the hallway. The inmate stood up and stepped out the door, and Banks walked behind him to the exit. Banks told Sanders to stop and face away and put his arms out to the side. Sanders complied. Banks said, "I'm going to pat you down. Don't move, okay?"

"Yes, sir."

He finished the pat down and walked him over to the other inmates and had him stop short of the other inmates. He went over to the other three inmates and asked them, "Any of you guys know this inmate?

They all looked at his and shook their heads. "No."

"What unit are you going to?"

One said F wing, and the others said the same.

"Show me your IDs?"

They pulled their IDs out and held them up. Banks was satisfied. "Thank you. Put them back in your pockets." Banks issued his instructions, "When you guys get to F wing stop and wait, okay?"

They nodded.

"Thank you. Step out into the corridor in one line and stop." The inmates complied. Banks told Sanders, "You fall in behind."

"Yes, sir."

"Okay, gentlemen, we're gonna walk single file down to RC. Hands behind your backs and no talking. Walk on the right side of the center lines. That's for us, Hoggs. If there is an alarm, stand against the wall to the right, face the wall with your hands behind your back, and don't move, okay?"

They all nodded.

Banks looked up and down the corridor and nodded to CO Kelly. Kelly keyed his radio. "Control, this is Infirmary Officer Kelly. I have an escort to RC. Can you turn on the light?"

"10-4, Kelly."

Red lights in the corridor ceiling illuminated. Banks yelled out, "Escort!"

In a softer voice, he told the line, "Okay, guys, let's take a walk."

He held up Sanders to let the group get a couple of yards ahead and told him, "Keep this distance from the group, okay?"

"Yes, sir."

The trek down the corridor was uneventful. When the line got to F wing, they stopped. Banks said, "Good job, guys. Hold here."

He walked around the group to the F wing entrance and saw F wing Officer White in the Officer's Station. Banks said, "I have three really mean guys for you."

White smiled. "Okay. I'll see if the maid has made their beds for them."

Banks turned back to the line. "Okay, guys, thanks for your cooperation." He walked over to Sanders and said, "Let's go."

Sanders went around the line and continued walking.

As they got to the corner of RC control, Banks directed Sanders to go left. They walked a few step more, and Banks told Sanders to stop and face the wall and told him, "Stay there for a sec."

Banks stepped over to the sergeant's office and saw Sergeant Perry at his desk. He cracked the door open and asked, "I have the vic from West Hall out here. You want to see him?"

Perry said, "Yeah, bring him in and sit him there," pointing to a chair.

"You want him cuffed?"

Perry shook his head. Banks nodded and stepped over to Sanders and said, "The sergeant wants to see you."

He led Sanders inside. Banks took a chair and turned it around and had Sanders sit straddling it, facing the back of the chair. He handed Perry his ID. Perry looked intently at Sanders as he entered and sat. He scanned his face and arms and saw several bruises and small cuts on his face. Perry looked at a report in his hand and put it on the desk. He began his process. "Mr. Sanders, I'm Sergeant Perry."

He paused, noticing Sanders's anxious face. "You seem like you're stressed out."

"Yes, sir," Sanders replied.

"I guess getting assaulted can do that."

"Yes, sir."

"I see that you got here two days ago."

"Yes, sir."

"That's a short time to piss off someone enough to get 'touched up.'"

Sanders's eyes wandered unfocused.

"What did you do to make your cellie attack you?"

"I told him what I did?"

"You mean your crime?" Perry asked. "Yes, sir."

Perry smiled knowingly and paused. "Let me guess: it was a niece or nephew that you got friendly with."

Sanders expression dimmed. "A neighbor's son."

"So you told your cellie that you molested a boy?" Banks was taking the conversation in.

"Yes, sir."

"Why did you tell him?"

"He was asking me where I was from and why I was here, so I told him."

Perry half smiled in concern. "I guess no one ever told you about prison. The inmates don't take kindly to child molesters and are bound by an unwritten code to assault or kill them."

"No, but he guy seemed like he didn't like it, but he didn't say anything until he came back from yard yesterday."

"Well, he probably told one of his homies your crime, and they told him what was expected." Perry paused, looking again at Sanders's face. "Is your face the only injuries?"

"Yes, sir, mostly."

Perry read some more on the report on his desk. He continued, "You're damn lucky that's all he did. And he probably may get a talking to for not doing more damage or for not taking you out completely. I see that your cellie is new also. You're lucky he wasn't an old number, or you would be in the morgue."

Perry leaned back in his chair, took a breath, then leaned his elbows on the desk. "Okay. Except for putting you in Ad Seg until you are sent to your assigned institution, I only have one course of action, and you get to choose."

Sanders asked, "What is that?"

"You mean Ad Seg?"

He nodded.

"In Ad Seg, you get little contact with anyone and don't see the outdoors, except maybe three times a week for about an hour each, and no physical contact with any visitors, if you get any. And if you continue that direction, you'll probably have to do your six years locked up twenty-three hours a day."

"What's the other choice?" he asked.

Perry continued, "What I can do is put you in a unit that has a different yard schedule, that doesn't have contact with the unit you were in, to help keep you safe. But that will only work if you don't tell anyone of your crime. You'll have to make up some story about the exact town you're from and that you burglarized some houses or sold drugs, something you can stick with for the rest of your time inside."

Sanders sat silently for a minute. "I'd like you put me in another unit."

"Okay, but you gotta do what I said." Sanders nodded.

Perry looked up at Banks. "Banks, put him in that holding cage right outside the door, and can you write me a 154 to get him to G wing?"

Banks replied. "Got it, Sarge. You want his 7219, or you want me to bring it back with the cell move?"

"Bring it back with the 154. Oh, and"—looking at Sanders, asked, "I guess you didn't make it to chow this morning?"

Sanders said, "No, sir."

Turning back to Banks, Perry continued, "See if you can rustle up a sack lunch for him also."

Banks nodded. He told Sanders to stand up and come with him out the door. He complied. Banks took him out of the office and over to the holding cage, unlocked it, and had him step in, then locked it. Banks told Sanders, "Okay, I'm gonna pick up two sack lunches for you because you'll probably miss lunch time in your new unit."

Banks paused and spoke softly to Sanders, "While you're in this cage, don't tell anyone what happened to you or what unit you are going to. Tell them you don't know. You gotta lie to stay alive, got it?"

"Yes, sir."

Banks added, "Just a suggestion: don't use the 'yes, sir' too much. I know you want to be polite, but it may not serve you too well in the inmate world, and use it sparingly with staff. A 'thanks, CO' will go a long way."

"Yes...uh...thanks, CO."

INCIDENTS WAITING TO HAPPEN

The B side entrance gate slid open, and Officer Porter stepped through, and the gate closed behind him. He walked down a slight slope to the yard complex entrance and down a hall past the inmate visiting room. Not being a visiting day, it was empty. He continued to the control room. He put his ID into the slot under the window. Officer Shaw took the ID to verify its owner. Shaw said, "Thank you, Porter," and pressed a button and a door slid open.

Porter went through, and the door closed behind him. In front of him was another control room in an open area with large barred sally port gates on either side. Porter saw Officer Beaber in the control room and pointed to his left. Beaber nodded, and the large gate to the left slowly slid open. Porter walked through as soon as it was wide enough. Beaber stopped the gate and reversed it to slowly close it. This area was a fifteen-by-fifteen-foot sally port with a door on the far right corner. Porter stood at the exit door looking out the window in the door.

When the gate finally closed Porter shouted, "Yard 1 door!"

Momentarily, the lock on the door clicked, and Porter stepped out and closed the door.

The yard was rather large, maybe 150 yards long by sixty yards wide. He took in the inmate activity on the yard as he walked along the asphalt walkway next to the single-story building that contained various offices, a dorm, and dining hall. On the opposite side were five separate inmate housing units. The inmates housed there were Level II custody with lower security needs in open dorm living.

Several officers were spread out among the two hundred or so inmates on the yard. Porter slowed as he went toward Sergeant Paris, standing along the building, watching the yard. He stopped and spoke, "Afternoon, Sarge. Keeping the masses in line?"

Paris responded, "Yeah, so far, so good. Maybe the rest of the day will stay that way."

Porter added, "You keep this yard quiet, and I'll keep H Dorm under control."

Paris interjected, "Well, that dorm can get squirrely at times, but you can handle it."

Porter sighed and said as he started to walk, "I'll do what I can."

He continued past this yard complex to a narrower walkway past a medical complex. Onward, he walked to 3 yard, another large yard complex with five units of Level III inmates with higher custody and security needs living in cells. He continued to another single-story building and went into a door in the middle of the building. In there was a long hallway that connected to another yard on the opposite side.

Porter went down the hall to the sergeant's office to sign in for his shift. Sergeant Malfi was at the desk on the phone. Porter went to the desk and picked through pages of sign-in sheets and found one to write on.

Malfi hung up the phone and greeted Porter. "Walt is in the house!"

Porter said, "You know it."

They laughed together. Malfi said, "I signed that swap for Thursday."

Porter said, "Thanks, I'll get it out of my box."

Malfi started, "Okay," and was interrupted by the phone ringing. Porter silently waved bye and left the office.

Porter exited the building, turned right along the building, took a few steps, stopped at a locked double door, and knocked loudly on it. He turned toward the yard and noted the activity. Momentarily, he heard the lock on the door being turned. The door opened, and Officer Powell said, "Hey, Porter."

Porter stepped in and said, "What's up, Powell?" Powell said, "Nada."

Porter continued into the dorm. Powell locked the door and followed Porter up three steps to the officer's station that was more like a stage. Porter scanned the dorm and saw Officer Carson above him on the gun walk. He spied Officer Sanchez in the back of the dorm. Porter put his lunch box under a desk, turned to Powell and asked, "Anything going on?"

"Not much. Yard's out. Laundry and meds are back."

Powell paused. "I did notice inmate Ortega hanging out by the Border Brothers, though."

Porter squinted in thought. "You had any small talk with him?"

"Just the usual: 'How's it going?' I got a few vibes," Powell replied.

Porter said, "Okay, I'll keep an eye on him and his homie Munoz. Anyway, give me your stuff and get out of here."

Powell took off his equipment one piece at a time and gave it to Porter. Porter checked each piece, cuffs, baton, OC, keys, and radio and put them on his belt and holders. When the transaction was finished, they exchanged fist bumps, and Powell said, "Thanks for the early relief."

Porter said, "No problem.

Powell went down the steps with Porter following. When they got to the exit door, Porter took a key group off his belt and unlocked the door to let Powell out. He told Powell, "Later, guy."

Powell stepped out the door and said, "I see Rosa coming in."

Porter took a step out the door and saw Officer Rosa walking toward him. He held the door for Rosa and let him in and greeted him, "Hey, partner."

They slapped their hands together chest high. Porter closed and locked the door. They made their way to the officer's station.

Rosa put his lunch container under the desk and picked the microphone up off of the desk, looked to the back of the dorm, and spoke, "Officer Sanchez, honey, your relief is here."

Officer Sanchez looked up toward Rosa and smiled. He walked to the officer's station, up the steps, and blew a kiss at Rosa. "We're supposed to keep us a secret, sweetie," Sanchez stated.

Rosa said, "Oh, quit your whining and give me your stuff. You gotta pick up the kids at day care."

Sanchez said, "Okay, baby."

Rosa was taking the equipment from Sanchez and seriously asked, "Anything happening?"

Sanchez said, "Not sure. Can't get a handle on the tension I feel."

Rosa said, "Yeah, I felt that way yesterday too. Guess we'll find out eventually, or it will fix itself."

Porter was listening to the conversation and added, "Powell was saying that Ortega was hanging around the Border Brothers, so there may be something to it."

They heard the door open above on the gun walk. Officer Campbell came in to relieve Officer Carson on the gun walk. After a few moments, Carson left the gun walk. Campbell surveyed the dorm noting the normal and unusual activities between the inmates. She was getting a lay of the land, preparing a plan of action should something go down. She bemoaned the idiotic implementation of triple bunks that took visual control away from her and was even worse for the officers on the floor. Surely, normal bunk beds in housing units restrict the detection of nefarious activities along with the inmate lockers that obstruct an officers' view.

The change to stacking three beds severely hampered security and safety of inmates and staff. Inmates were generally not pleased with the move to place more inmates in open dorm units to address overcrowding. With only about two feet between the lower bunk and the middle bunk and the same between the middle and upper bunk, it is problematic for most inmates. A somewhat manageable eightyto a 120-man dorm was transformed to a 110- to 160-inmate population and the extra lockers to deal with. The powers that be should have to work a day in this environment with incidents waiting to happen.

Campbell looked down to the officer's station and caught Porter's eye. She held her hand to simulate talking on a phone. Porter understood and called up to the gun walk. Campbell answered the ring. "Campbell, H Dorm Gun."

Porter spoke, "Hey, Babs."

"Afternoon Rob," she replied. "You settled in?" he asked "Yeah, I'm doin' good," she said.

"Did Carson give you any 411 on the dorm?"

"He mentioned that some Border Brothers weren't getting along."

"Powell said Ortega was paling around with them. Seems the plot thickens," he surmised.

"Well, maybe they'll wait till after chow so they can get locked up on a full stomach," she suggested.

Porter said, "Great minds think alike."

She replied, "Oh, someone else has a great mind besides me?" Porter smirked and said, "Bye, Babs," and hung up.

Porter and Rosa infused themselves in their daily routine for the next couple of hours. Checking the showers and bathrooms for inappropriate activity and handing out soap and toilet paper was ongoing. Walking among their charges and making small talk was a continual endeavor to maintain a semblance of positive humanity yet realizing that there existed a line between being friendly and being friends.

Campbell was being her tenacious self, keeping a watchful eye on her staff below. Every gunner knows the importance keeping track of the staff, and the staff knows the importance of staying visible and letting the gunner know where they are.

Porter came back to the officer's station, and Rosa soon followed. They were preparing for the return of the inmates out on the yard to their housing units. Rosa was sitting on a chair at the desk, and Porter was sitting on the desk. They were exchanging information and pleasantries when "yard recall" was announced on the yard and on the radio. Rosa said, "I'll take the door."

He stood up and walked down the steps and over to the exit door and unlocked and opened it. He stood outside the door, waiting for the dorm inmates to return.

Anyone who spends time supervising inmates relies on their most valuable tool: correctional awareness, being aware of your surroundings and unusual activities. No one can give all the situations that may present a danger. Daily experience and the mental game of "What if this happens, what would I do?" helps prepare for the unexpected. These experienced staff members continue to hone these skills daily.

Rosa checked each inmate before he allowed them to enter. Those he didn't recognize by sight, he would ask for an ID card, and those he did recognize, he allowed to pass. If there was anything suspicious—i.e., cuts, bruises, bulges under clothing, or bulky clothing—he would check it out.

Inside, Porter and Campbell were watching the flow of inmates, noting any unusual interactions. After a few minutes, Rosa saw that the last of the inmates had returned to their units, and the yard staff was making their way back to the main building. He stepped back in and closed and locked the door and proceeded to the officer's station.

Porter was in front of the podium, talking to an inmate. He went up the steps to a locker and took out a roll of toilet paper, went back to the inmate, and gave it to him. He went over toward the bathroom and shower area and stood watching the inmate movement.

Rosa was seated in one of the chairs at the desk. He was writing in the Daily Activity Report (DAR), logging the time of yard return. He picked up the phone and rang above to Campbell. "H Dorm Gun, Campbell," she stated.

Rosa asked, "Just checking for the DAR, if you had any discrepancies in your equipment."

"Nope. All good," she replied. Rosa said, "Thanks," and hung up.

Rosa swiveled aimlessly in his chair, watching the unit for several minutes. He stood up and walked down into the left middle of the dorm. He walked by several triple bunks, taking in the inmates' activity and observing in open lockers the clothing, shoes, and food the inmate may have. Some inmates were sleeping or reading in their bed.

He veered off to the left side of the dorm to some tables and TV viewing area. Some inmates were playing cards or writing. He continued around to other side of the dorm, past Porter by the shower area, and then back to the officer's station. He sat down in one of the chairs, reached into a drawer, and picked up a dorm count sheet and clipped it to a clipboard.

Porter looked at his watch and walked back to the officer's podium and sat next to Rosa. "Guess it's about time for count," Porter said.

"Yep, you want to count, or me?" Rosa said. Porter took the clipboard and said, "I'll do it."

They sat for several minutes, talking and watching the dorm, waiting for the radio announcement for count time. Soon, they were not disappointed. The radio crackled. "Control to all units, it's count time, count time."

Porter picked up the dorm mic and announced, "Okay, it's count time. Back to your bunks. Standing count."

Most of the inmates were already at their bunks, and the rest scurried to theirs.

In order to facilitate a standing count, each inmate is required to stand in order to ensure a count of live-breathing flesh. In this case, due to the closeness of the bunks, the inmate on the top bunk could sit up on the bed, and the other two would stand together at one end of the bunks. They were not to move until the count was cleared.

Rosa stood up and positioned himself in the center of the podium with a clear view of the entire dorm, as did Campbell from the dorm gun walk. This vigilance was to ensure that any inmate didn't move or double back to take the place of another missing inmate, thus being counted twice.

Porter stood up and walked down the steps to the left side of the dorm to the first set of triple bunks. Porter went by each triple bunk, marking on the count sheet a check by each bunk number and letter: *B* for bottom, *M* for middle, and *U* for upper. When he finished his trek through the maze of bunks, he returned to the podium. The inmates remained at their bunk area, only allowed to sit or lie on their bed until told they could move about.

Porter sat down and picked up a large clear plastic-covered bed chart attached to cardboard. On it were the names and numbers of the inmates in the unit written in wax pencil. There was a number, 106, written at the top.

Porter compared the bed chart with the count sheet he had done. Using an adding machine, he entered numbers and finished the calculation. He rechecked his figures and seemed satisfied. He picked up the phone and dialed. Porter listened and spoke. "Porter with H Dorm count." He paused, then spoke. "H Dorm count, 106."

After another pause he said, "Thank you." He turned to Rosa and said, "It's clear."

He saw Campbell looking down and gave her a thumbs-up. Porter punched two holes at the top of the count sheet and put the sheet into a folder. Rosa walked back to the desk and sat down. They sat watching the dorm. Rosa asked, "Walt, did you see the game last night?"

Porter replied, "I caught the last quarter when they blew a twelve-point lead. Should have known Curry would catch fire. Oh well."

Rosa added, "Such is life."

The radio came alive. "Control to the Watch Commander and all units, the count is clear. Count is clear at 1648 hours."

Rosa picked up the dorm mic and said, "Count's clear."

The inmates, now allowed to move, were getting ready for chow. Some went over toward the exit door and sat at tables, waiting. The radio announced, "Building 13 release for chow."

"13 copies."

The traffic on the radio was busy for about twenty minutes with back and forth announcements of "13 coming back,"

"Building 10, send them," and finally, "H Dorm, release for chow."

Rosa responded, "H Dorm copies."

Porter walked down to the door and unlocked and opened it. Some inmates had already lined up and hurried out. Most of the others meandered out the door. Porter and Rosa surveyed the dorm and noticed that all of the inmates had gone to chow. Rosa keyed his mic. "This is H Dorm. You got 'em all."

"Copy, H Dorm," was the response.

Porter closed and locked the door and said, "Guess all of them decided to eat."

Rosa said, "Yeah, looks that way. Must be burgers tonight." Porter looked on the wall at the schedule for dinner and said,

"Yep, you're right—hamburgers and mac and cheese."

Porter and Rosa walked back to the desk. Porter stated, "Well, you think we should eat our lunches now or take a chance that nothing happens and we can eat later?"

Rosa thought for a moment. Campbell caught the conversation and chimed in, "Well, I'm gonna eat now and snack later. Just sayin'."

Rosa and Porter laughed. Rosa said, "Well, I think that's the plan."

Porter said, "Yep, me too."

Out on the yard, Sergeant Malfi and Yard S&E Layton were standing close to the wall in between the entrance and exit doors of the dining hall. Yard officers Sihdu and Parker ushered in the last of the H Dorm inmates into the dining hall and followed them in. Officer Layton stepped over and locked the door behind them.

The inmates followed the well-ingrained feeding process, channeling single file through the iron pipe-rail-lined walkway. At the opening in the wall of steel sheeting of the steam line, each inmate would retrieve a tray of food and continue toward a table with canisters and pour a beverage of choice. Inmates could then find a stainless steel table and be seated at one of the attached four seats. On the gun walk twenty-five feet above, Officer Lopez stood ready to identify and, if needed, quell any disturbance.

Sihdu and Parker occasionally wandered around and in between the tables simply to show a presence. Sihdu took special note that the chow hall was unusually quiet. As either of the officers approached a table, the inmate conversation would lessen. All but three tables were full, with a noticeable exception: Inmate Ortega was seated alone at a table near the exit with his back to the wall. Sihdu, of course,

took note and went over to Ortega and leaned against the table and watched the chow from there. He glanced down at Ortega and said somewhat softly, "How's it going, guy?"

Ortega half smiled and nodded his head. He was almost finished eating, while most of the other inmates were less than half done with their meals. Sihdu said, "Guess you prefer to eat alone."

He restated in his best Spanish, "Quiere comer solamente?" Ortega nodded. "Yes, si."

"Tiene algun peligro?" he asked if he was in danger.

Ortega slightly shook his head no then slightly nodded yes. Sihdu asked his name.

"Como se llama?"

Ortega said softly, "Ortega."

Sihdu smiled for show and said nonchalantly, "You'll be okay, guy," and casually walked away. He went over and stood near the steam line and watched to see if any inmates were looking at Ortega.

Parker strolled over to Sihdu and said, "You noticed how quiet the chow is too, huh?"

Sihdu said, "Yeah. Check the inmates out to see who might be watching inmate Ortega sitting by himself."

Parker said, "I saw you say something to him. He must be alone for a reason."

Sihdu countered, "Yeah, he's in trouble."

They stood watching the inmates, taking note of any suspicious looks from other inmates. They talked in sort of a whisper to each other for a couple of minutes. Parker asked, "Are those border brothers at that third table by the drinks?"

Sihdu said, "Yeah, I think so."

"I noticed the two on the right glancing at Ortega and talking to each other," Parker added.

"We probably should check them out when they leave," Sihdu said. "Okay, if you want to pull Ortega aside, I'll get Layton to help me pat down those two," Parker said.

Seeing that the inmates were mostly finished with chow, Parker went to the exit door and knocked. Sihdu walked over to Ortega's table and motioned to Ortega to stand up and dump his tray.

Layton opened the door, and Sihdu escorted Ortega out first and walked him over to Sergeant Malfi, who was standing on the yard.

The other inmates automatically randomly stood up and headed to the exit, dumping the contents of their trays into trash cans and exiting the chow hall.

Parker told Layton he was going to pick out a couple of inmates for pat downs. Layton nodded. Sihdu told Ortega to give him his ID card and stay put while he spoke to Sergeant Malfi. "Hey, Sarge, Ortega was sitting by himself in chow and nodded he was in danger when I asked him," Sihdu related.

Malfi asked, "He say who or why?"

Sihdu said, "I didn't ask him anything else. Just wanted to get him out safe."

He gave Malfi Ortega's ID card. Malfi stepped over to Ortega. "Mr. Ortega, you understand English?"

Ortega said, "Si, yes."

"Are you concerned for your safety?" he asked. "Yes."

"Why? What's going on?"

Ortega was hesitant. "Some people might want to hurt me."

"Why do they want to hurt you?"

Ortega paused. "I didn't want to hurt somebody?"

"You mean they want you to make a hit?" Malfi pressed on. "Who wants you make the hit, and who do they want you to hit?"

Ortega became anxious and shook his head. Malfi pressed on.

"You know how this goes. I can't protect you if you can't give me who wants the hit or who it's on and why."

Ortega thought for a moment, "It's on Becerra…for a gambling debt."

"Becerra in your dorm?" Ortega nodded.

"Okay," Malfi said and turned to Sihdu. "Let's put him in a holding cage, and I'll talk to him after I call H Dorm."

Sihdu nodded. Malfi said in a quiet voice, "Be careful. He might want to assault staff to get locked up."

Sihdu nodded. He put handcuffs on Ortega, and they followed Malfi toward the main building.

When all of the inmates had returned to H Dorm, Porter closed and locked the door. He went over to the officer's station and sat down next to Rosa. The phone rang, and Porter answered, "Porter, H Dorm."

"Hey, Walt, Malfi. I have Ortega here in my office. You have an Inmate Becerra in your dorm?"

Porter reached over to the unit bed chart and searched the names. He said, "Yeah, there is a Border Brother in H-79 up."

Malfi said, "See if you can quietly scoop him up and put him in a cage. Seems Ortega was told to make a hit on him for a gambling debt. Call me back when you have him. I'll call the gunner and let them know."

"Got it, Sarge."

Porter hung up the phone and quietly told Rosa the situation and pointed to Becerra's picture on the dorm chart. Rosa casually stood up and said, "I'll go around the right side, and you can take the middle."

Porter nodded. He waited until Rosa had stepped down to the floor and easily got up and walked down the steps.

The phone on the gun walk rang. "Campbell, H Dorm Gun."

"Campbell, Malfi. Porter and Rosa are going to get Becerra H-79 upper. He may be the target of a hit."

"Okay, Sarge," she replied and hung up.

When Porter got to Becerra's bunk, he didn't see him. He caught Rosa's attention and shook his head. Rosa shook his head also. Rosa checked out the tables by the TV area on his side of the dorm. Porter headed back toward the front to check the shower area for Becerra. Porter finally saw Becerra in the bathroom/shower area and head nodded to Rosa toward the shower area.

Becerra was coming out of the bathroom/shower area. He tossed his shirt over his shoulder. Suddenly, he moaned and grabbed the side of his head and began dodging and defending with his arms and hands. Inmate Munoz was swinging a sock with something heavy in inside of it and attacking Becerra incessantly with blows to his upper torso. Porter and Rosa saw the attack and both sprinted toward it. Both officers yelled, "Get down!"

The entire dorm, hearing the command, lay or sat down on the floor or bunks Rosa pressed his alarm device. When Munoz saw them getting close, he stopped the attack tossed the sock away. Becerra turned toward Munoz and hit him in his face. Munoz turned away and lay facedown on the ground. Becerra had cuts and abrasions on his face and arms. He turned and started kicking Munoz in his side. Porter got to the incident first and told Becerra to get down, and he complied.

Rosa looked up at Campbell and asked, "You see anything else?" She was holding the 40 mm baton launcher at her hip and said,

"No, that's all I see."

The radio broke its silence. "Control to all units, there is an alarm in H Dorm, Watch Commander, you copy?"

"Watch 1 copies."

The entrance door lock clicked, and several staff carefully entered the dorm and spread out in the dorm to ensure that there were no other problems and all the inmates were lying on the ground. Rosa keyed up his radio and said, "Control, this is Officer Rosa, the alarm is an inmate assault. Show us a Code 4 for now. I need a supervisor and medical."

"Control copies."

There was an overlapping radio message heard, "Control, Sergeant Malfi is 10-97."

"Control copies."

Sergeant Malfi came through the door and went over to Porter and asked, "You guys okay? You hurt?"

Porter shook his head and said, "No, I'm okay."

Rosa said, "No, when we got close, Munoz got down, and Becerra got down when we told him."

"Which one is Becerra?" Malfi asked.

Porter pointed to Becerra. Malfi said, "Couldn't get to him in time, huh?"

Layton came up to Rosa and Porter and asked, "Just these two?" Porter said, "Yeah. You want to cuff this one"—pointing to

Becerra—"and I'll cover you."

Layton said nothing and knelt down and searched Becerra and handcuffed him and left him on the ground. Rosa said, "I'll get Munoz."

Porter said, "Okay, I'll cover you too."

Rosa searched and cuffed Munoz and left him on the ground also.

MTA Mackie came into the dorm, looked around, and went over to Malfi. "What you need, Sarge?" he asked.

"See if these guys are okay to escort out," Malfi said.

Mackie went to each inmate to evaluate their conditions. Layton told Porter, pointing to Becerra, "That's one of the guys Parker said was eyeing Ortega in the chow hall, and we pulled them out of the chow hall and patted them down."

Porter said, "Yeah? It's an odd scenario. I'm curious to see how this plays out."

Mackie finished his evaluations and said, "Becerra has cuts and scrapes, but he says he can walk. Munoz can walk to medical also."

Malfi said, "Okay. Layton, you and Parker escort these two separately to medical and put them in separate rooms."

Layton stood Becerra up and escorted him out of the unit. Parker stood Munoz up. Rosa asked Parker if he could transfer the cuffs on Munoz so he could get his assigned handcuffs back. Parker took his cuffs out and put them on Munoz and removed Rosa's cuffs and gave them back to Rosa. Parker left the dorm with Munoz.

Porter told Malfi, "Sarge, Munoz was hitting Becerra with a sock that had something heavy in it and tossed it over there." He pointed to the shower area. "You want me to get it or someone else?"

"You have an evidence bag in your desk?" Malfi asked. Porter said, "Yes, I do."

"Okay, put it in a bag and keep it for chain of custody. ISU should be here in a few minutes. If not, you can log it in later," Malfi directed.

Porter went up to his desk to get an evidence bag. He went back and picked up the sock, felt it, looked inside, and saw a combination lock. He put the sock with its contents in the bag and put it a pocket in his protective vest. Porter went over to Malfi and said, "There's a combination lock in the sock."

Malfi said, "Guess he was serious. The sock must have been a spur-of-the-moment choice of weapons. ISU can check the number and see whose it is."

Rosa walked around the area looking for anything that could be evidence and didn't find anything. Malfi motioned the two to follow him over to the desk. He said, "Okay, if there's nothing else, I look forward to your reports," and looked up to Campbell and said, "I know you're listening, Campbell. You've got a report too."

Campbell smiled and gave a thumbs-up.

Malfi turned to the staff in the dorm and said, "Okay, guys, let's get back to our jobs."

The staff quickly left the dorm, and Malfi followed them out. Porter locked the door and walked over to Becerra's bunk area. Rosa cordoned off the shower area with crime scene tape from their desk drawer.

The entrance door lock snapped, and Investigative Service Unit (ISU) Officers Rader and Howell came into the dorm and locked the door. Rosa smiled and met them at the officer's station. Rosa said, "Glad to see you guys. Would you like to take over the investigation, please?"

Porter walked up and said, "Yeah, please."

Howell said, "You wimps. Afraid of getting your hands dirty?" Rosa said, "But you guys are sooooo good at this."

Howell turned to Rader and said, "See how worthless these POS are. They're always trying to butter us up to get out of real work."

Powell smiled and said, "Love you, guys. Let's give you a rundown on what we have and see what you need from us."

Howell said, "Okay, let's have it."

Malfi walked down the hallway toward his office. He paused at the Lieutenant's office and peeked in. His secretary, Jackson, saw him at the door, and he said, "If you're looking for the Lieu, she went to the custody complex.

Malfi said, "Thanks, Paul. I'll catch her later." He turned and went down the hall and into his office. He keyed his radio. "Yard 4, S-1."

"Go for Yard 4," was the response.

"Can you 10-19 my office?" Malfi asked. "10-4 in two."

Malfi sat down at his desk and pressed a key on a computer keyboard, and the screen lit up. He typed in a password and scrolled to his desired file and opened it. Officer Sihdu came into the office. "What cha need, Sarge?"

Malfi said, "Can you bring me Ortega out of the cage?"

"Will do," Sihdu said and left.

Malfi continued typing for several minutes. He picked up the phone and dialed it, waited for an answer, and said, "Malfi, is Parker close by? Okay thanks."

Malfi waited then continued, "Parker, does Munoz have any life threatening injuries?" He paused again. "Okay, how about Becerra?" He listened for a moment and said, "Yeah, could have been a lot worse." He continued, "Okay, just getting a little prelim for my 837.

You and Layton, don't forget your part Cs."

He listened for a few seconds then said, "Okay, thanks," and hung up.

Sihdu came to the door and said, "I've got Ortega." Malfi said, "Bring him in."

Sihdu stepped out of the door and brought Ortega in. Malfi said, "Ortega, have a seat."

Sihdu took a chair and turned it around and placed it backwards with the seat facing away from the desk. He had Ortega straddle the seat and sit down facing Malfi. Malfi began, "Ortega, I'm a little intrigued and confused. I don't really need you to say anything, but let me know if I get something wrong." Malfi paused and saw Ortega nod his head.

"I checked your file and saw that you've been down for six years and have an EPRD in five months, so I'm not surprised that you don't want to add any time to that and jeopardize your possible parole date."

Ortega seemed to agree with Malfi's summary.

Malfi continued, "I see that you have been somewhat aligned with the Nortenos, although you came from Temecula. The Structure isn't as strict as the Southerns are. I probably would do the same thing if I wanted to survive in here." Malfi paused.

"I am curious about why a hit for a simple gambling debt would be sanctioned by the 'shot caller' on the yard. My guess is that the hit was over drugs, someone stepping on the red rag's territory." Malfi stopped and looked at Ortega. "How am I doing?"

Ortega somewhat nodded. Malfi continued, "Okay, ISU can sort out the effects of this incident, but you probably heard the alarm earlier and know that it was in your dorm. But you might want to know that your homie Munoz might have saved you. You'll probably have to spend the rest of your time in lockup until you, hopefully, parole."

Ortega looked at Malfi and said, "I understand, sergeant. Thank you for telling me about Munoz."

Malfi said, "Well, you'll probably see him in Ad Seg or an SNY somewhere." He paused. "Good luck."

He looked up at Sihdu and said, "You can put him back in holding until the Lt. decides what to do with him or until ISU picks him up."

Sihdu tapped Ortega on the shoulder, and he stood up. Sihdu walked Ortega to the door and stopped and said to Malfi, "It seems that every day there are incidents waiting to happen."

Malfi nodded.

SPILLOVER

Officers Riley and Belders walked up to the A-Yard entrance gate. Riley spoke loudly at the speaker box near the gate, "A-Yard Gate."

After a few seconds, the lock on the gate snapped, and Riley pushed it open, and they both walked through and closed the gate. They continued a short distance down the asphalt walkway by a long single-story building. They turned and walked into the yard custody office and went into the sergeant's office. Sergeant Ivy was at the desk on the phone. The officers picked up a clipboard, and each thumbed through the papers and signed in for their shift. They nodded to Ivy, who returned their nod, turned and left the office, and stepped out of the custody office onto the yard.

They both headed across the yard toward the housing units. As they walked, they were mindful of the yard activity. They noticed there were four officers from ISU also on the yard. There were several hundred inmates exercising on the yard; playing baseball, basketball, tennis; and walking and running on the track path. The yard was not the normal flat layout. There were gentle slopes down to the entrances to the buildings.

Belders asked Riley, "You in 3 control?"

"Yep, and you're in 5 control," Riley countered. "You go check out the truck yesterday?" Riley asked.

"Yeah. It's a little used, but it will suit my needs. Just need something to haul shit with when I need it," Belders said.

"You said it was a six, right?" Riley said.

"Yeah, with the extended cab to put all the other crap I don't use in it."

Riley laughed. "I know what you mean."

They neared Building 3, and Riley gave Belders a fist bump. "Okay, Bro. I'll call you in a bit," Riley said as he peeled off to his building.

Riley went down a slight slope to the asphalt entrance of Building 3 and walked up to the door. He spoke loudly up to the second floor window, "Yard door staff."

Momentarily, the door slid open. Riley stepped in and stood by another door immediately inside and waited for the yard door to close. He looked up through thick glass ports into the control room above. Officer Casey looked down at Riley and stepped over to a panel and pushed a button that snapped open the lock on the door. Riley stepped in to a small entry and closed the door behind him. When the door closed, the lock on the next door snapped, and Riley opened it, went through, and closed the door behind him. He walked up the steps into control.

Officer Casey was standing at the control panel, watching the housing unit floor area and tiers. The thick glass with thick bars offered an unobstructed 270-degree view of the two tiers of the unit. The floor of the control booth had interspersed thick glass and ports to observe the entrance hallway below and also the offices directly below. Walking on the glass areas takes a little getting used to.

Riley spoke, "Casey, what's up, guy?"

"Same ole, same ole," he replied.

Riley sat his lunch down under the control panel and went over to a wall and took a clipboard off. He immediately began the routine of checking the various miscellaneous inventory items and the critical inventory: keys, radios, air packs, batons, and chemical agents. He ensured the mechanical operation of the handcuffs, waist chains, grenade launchers, mini 14 and accounted for all of the munitions. He went over and picked up an activity log and read a couple of pages. When he finished, he went over to Casey and put his hand on his shoulder and said, "Okay, Paul, you ready to get out of here?"

Casey smiled. "You kidding? I love it here."

"Right," Riley said. "Anything going on?"

Casey paused. "You know, it seems that ALL of the Bloods went out to the yard. That's a little odd. We checked the other units, and theirs are out too. We told the squad, and they're concerned."

Riley replied, "Yeah, Belders and I noticed the squad on the yard on the way in."

"We checked B and C yards to see if their Bloods were on the yard, and only C yard's Bloods were all on the yard," Casey added.

"Seems like something might be going down. Guess time will tell," Riley said. "Okay, dude, inventory is cool, so get out of here before something kicks off and you are locked in. We'll deal with what happens."

Casey nodded. "Thanks, Frank."

Riley pushed a button to unlock the door below. He watched as Casey went down the steps to the first door. Riley unlocked the series of doors, and Casey eventually stepped out of the unit onto the yard.

Riley looked around the housing unit below and located his two unit officers Faris and Gipson in the dayroom. There were only about fifteen to twenty inmates on the dayroom floor.

Riley went over to the control panel and sat down. He opened up the Daily Activity Report (DAR) log and read a few sections and wrote a few lines in it and closed it.

Riley slowly walked around the control room and across the perimeter, scanning the activities of the inmates and staff. Occasionally, an inmate would catch his attention, and he would open or close a cell door for the inmate. He walked to the window that looked out onto the yard to watch those activities. His meandering in the control room broke up the monotony of the job. That activity kept his mind in a ready mode to act when needed. Eventually, he went back to the panel and sat down. He picked up the phone and dialed. "Belders 5 control," was the answer.

Riley spoke, "JB, did I wake you?"

"What do you think, you piece of shit," Belders chuckled. Riley laughed. "Who you working with?"

"Bartley and Davis," he replied. "Regina Davis?" Riley asked. "Yep."

"Well, your floor cops have it handled then, so you can go back to sleep," Riley quipped.

"Sure, I'd do that, but you'd wake me up again."

"So...did all your Bloods go out to the yard?" Riley asked. "Yeah, and of course all the Southerns too."

"Yeah, they always go to the yard," Riley added.

"You think there might be some fallout from the Folsom Sureno attack on the Bloods last week?" Belders asked.

"Could be. Maybe they'll keep it on the yard," Riley added. "That would be the most likely scenario," Belders said. "Anyway, if you get that truck, I'll come check it out." Belders replied, "Might get it tomorrow. I'll see."

"Okay, JB. Call you later," Riley said.

Belders replied, "Alright, later." Belders hung up the phone and walked over to the yard window and stared out for a minute or so, then he went to the windows overlooking the dayroom. He stopped to watch Davis talk to an inmate through the cell door on the second tier.

The inmate population has, as a matter of deliberate agreement, had a long standing practice of dividing up the yard areas by race and further divide those areas by gang affiliation. Those areas are normally determined in each initial opening of an institution and the first opening of each yard. The inmate group that has the numbers or the power can "claim" their area, and what is left goes to the next in the hierarchy.

As time goes on, the population settles into the routine. Changes and newly added areas are usually made by a "meet and confer" of the group's leaders, shot callers. As the makeup of the prison population changes, so do the areas used by a particular group. Most of the changes are by amicable agreement, but if not, violent methods are used. Each institution is its own "animal." It is also cognizant of other institution's inmate population activities. The disagreements at one institution, or "war," can infect some or all the institutions in the state.

Bloods-affiliated inmates Frasier and Moore sat on a bench along the walkway in front of Building 5. They were watching the Southern inmates playing basketball. They were seated near a water fountain. A short distance away, in three different directions, were groups of two or three Bloods. Unless they are playing together, more than three in a group draws attention of staff and other inmates.

Normally, each gang has a lookout posted during their group's activity, basketball, etc., and a member doesn't walk alone. In times of heightened awareness, staff is particularly vigilant.

Due to the Southern-Bloods incident at Folsom a week ago, there were two pairs of security squad members walking the yard to reinforce the other 3 yard staff. Hopefully, this show of presence might derail any violent confrontation.

On the other side of the yard, two Bloods sat at each of two tables that were located in front and below the yard gun observation booth high on the complex building. Officer Chang was manning the yard gun post. He was aware of the possibility of an incident occurring. He watched two black inmates that had made it around the yard making contact with each small group of other black inmates. He saw Squad Officers Boyd and Polk standing in front of the custody complex. He reached over and picked up the phone and dialed. "A-Yard Sergeant Ivy," was the answer.

"Ivy, Chang."

"What's up, Chang?"

"Sarge, I see a couple of squad cops out by your office. Can you get one to come in so I can talk to both of you on speaker?"

Ivy said, "Sure, hold on."

He picked up his radio and keyed it up. "Squad 3, A-Yard Sergeant."

The ISU officer on the yard responded, "Go for, Squad 3."

"Can you 10-21 my office?" Ivy asked.

"10-4 in two," was the response.

Squad 3, Officer Boyd was near the sergeant's office and went in to the complex entrance and then into the sergeant's office. Sergeant Ivy was sitting at the desk.

Boyd asked, "What you need, Sarge?

Ivy pressed the speaker button on his phone and said, "Chang, A-Yard Gun is on speaker."

Boyd nodded and said, "Hey, Chang, Boyd. What's up?"

"I have two black inmates making rounds on the yard," Chang said.

"Yeah, Polk and I saw them too. Seems like they are delivering instructions. We haven't seen them pass off anything yet."

"I saw one of them with my binoculars give a piece of paper to one of the guys at the table near the Indian sweat grounds."

Boyd replied, "Good catch. Polk and I will check them out. Thanks, Chang."

Chang said, "You got it. Guess I'll announce yard recall in about five minutes. Give you guys a chance to get back out to where you think you should be."

"Okay, later," Boyd said and hung up the phone.

Boyd said, "Well, Sarge, guess I'll check it out. Thanks for the call."

Ivy said, "Yep." Ivy stood up. "I'll walk out with you."

They both left the office and went back out to the yard. Boyd went over to Polk and told him what Chang had said. Boyd saw the other squad officers on the other end of the yard. He keyed his radio mic. "Squad 5, Tac 2."

"Go ahead on Tac 2," Weaver said.

Boyd said, "Chang said he saw inmates Carter and Jones hand a piece of paper to the guys at the table by the sweat lodge. You guys wanna check 'em out? Oh, and yard recall in four mics."

Weaver said, "10-4."

Weaver and his partner Wallace walked casually over toward the table by the sweat lodge. They carefully approached the inmates sitting at the table. Weaver spoke to the inmates, "Hey, guys, can I see your IDs?"

The inmates reached into their pockets and handed them to Weaver, who said, "Thank you."

He looked at them and said, "Pratt and Collins."

He turned to one of the inmates. "Pratt, could you stand up? I want to pat you down." He handed the IDs to Wallace.

Pratt asked, "What's up 5-0? Didn't do nothin'." Weaver said, "Just my routine searches."

Pratt stood up, and Weaver directed him to face away. Wallace stepped to the side to have a view of Collins and the search process. As Weaver searched, he handed his findings to Wallace: a hat and a handkerchief. When he finished, he gave Pratt back his property. "Thank you, Pratt."

Pratt sat back down. He turned to Collins and asked him to stand, and he stood up. At that moment, the yard speaker came alive. "Yard recall. Yard recall."

Collins said, "Can I go back to my house?"

Weaver said, "In a minute. Let me pat you down first."

Collins shook his head impatiently and turned around and put his hands out to his sides. Weaver took a hat off of Collins and handed it to Wallace. Wallace searched it and found a folded piece of paper in the headband. Weaver continued to search Collins. Wallace unfolded the paper and read it.

Recall Yard Gun.

As inmates slowly gathered belongings and wandered off of recreational areas, the Southern inmates on the basketball court filtered off the court. On the other side of the yard in front of the yard gun overlook, several black inmates began yelling and grabbing each other in wrestling holds, hitting each other, and rolling on the ground.

Yard Gunner Chang saw the commotion and assessed the situation. He pressed the yard alarm button, grabbed the 40 mm grenade launcher that contained rubber baton rounds and yelled out the window to the inmates below, "Get down. Get down."

The inmates continued to fight. He fired down at the feet of the group and reloaded another rubber round and fired again. Several yard staff came toward the incident and waited for direction from the yard gunner Chang.

Sergeant Ivy, Boyd, and Polk were in front of the custody office and sprinted to the scene. Ivy keyed his radio while running and announced the incident. In Building 5, Belders was watching the inflow of inmates into his unit when he heard the yard alarm. Riley in Building 3 also heard the alarm. The floor staff in both housing units ordered the inmates to stop and lie down. Belders and Riley closed both doors in their building sally ports.

Inmates Frasier and Moore each retrieved a weapon from the ground next to the bench they were sitting at and ran toward the Southern Hispanics drinking at a fountain. Not far away, Weaver and Wallace were still dealing with Inmates Pratt and Collins. Inmate Pratt, on hearing the yelling and shots from the yard gun area, stood up and began to run toward the drinking fountain. Collins, still being searched, shook loose from Weaver's grasp. Wallace and Weaver also heard the incident in the yard gun area, and as Collins and Pratt ran the other direction, Wallace and Weaver instinctively pulled out their batons.

Near the end of Building 5, some Southern inmates were at a drinking fountain. Inmates Frasier and Moore ran up to one of the several Southern inmates and began slashing and stabbing any target of opportunity. Within a few seconds, several black inmates joined the attack, brandishing their own weapons. When Inmates Collins and Pratt finally got there, they began to hit, kick, and hold Southern inmates so they could be stabbed or slashed.

The inmates in Buildings 5 and 3 were all lying down and under supervision of the staff. Belders went to the yard window and saw the melee toward the end of his building. He picked up his Mini- 14, held it at port arms, and took in the various assaults taking place. Riley also was at his window facing the yard. He too held his Mini-14 at port arms. Squad Officers Weaver and Wallace ran across the yard toward the fighting at the fountain. They saw the serious injuries being inflicted. They yelled at the combatants to stop and get down to no avail. They each sprayed various attackers with OC pepper spray that had little effect. They each tossed a tear gas canister toward the inmates.

The inmates at the other end of the yard by the yard gun suddenly all lay facedown and put their hands out to their side. Chang raised his weapon to port arms and scanned the yard. He immediately noticed the skirmish at the other end of the yard. He and Sergeant Ivy noticed it at the same time. Chang called down to Ivy and pointed to the incident. Ivy said, "Damn, I see it. Chang, cover these guys, and I'll leave you two officers."

He pointed to two officers and said, "You two watch them. The rest of you, come with me."

He keyed his radio and notified control of the other incident. The pack ran with their leader to the other end of the yard. Except for the combatants, the other inmates on the yard were proned out. Wallace and Weaver circled to their left and met up with Sergeant Ivy, Boyd, and Polk. They positioned themselves just a little away from the incident and continuously ordered the inmates to stop.

Boyd and Polk each threw a tear gas canister at the group. Sergeant Ivy realized that the yard gun was occupied, and the only coverage was from the buildings. He had his group move their line away from the melee and parallel to the buildings. Sergeant Ivy called on the radio, "Building 5 control, we're clear and waiting."

In Building 5, Belders heard the radio transmission. He saw that the staff skirmish line was clear from harm. He saw several inmates with weapons attacking other inmates with weapons. He focused on one of the inmates on top of another stabbing at him. He took aim with the Mini-14 and took the shot. The attacker fell over.

One Hispanic inmate began to run in front of Building 5 with a black inmate in chase. As they neared the front of Building 4, Riley saw the chase. He didn't see any weapon in the Black inmate's hands. He had changed his weapon of choice to the 40 mm with a multiple baton round. The black inmate was getting close to his target. The Hispanic ran up to Building 3 with the other inmate in chase. Riley yelled, "Stop! Get down!"

The Hispanic inmate complied, but the black inmate continued toward the inmate on the ground. Riley took a bead at the black inmate and fired. The rounds landed at the feet of the inmate and bounced up, striking him in the upper torso. That made him change his mind, and he stopped. Riley reloaded and called to the inmate, "Back away and lie down facing away, NOW."

The inmate complied.

After Belders saw the inmate fall from his shot, he saw that the other inmates had ceased their attack. Sergeant Ivy took control of the scene. Staff responded from the other yards and units to assist in containing the incident. Medical was on scene, attending to the shot inmate and other injured. One by one, the inmates were identified, cuffed up, and removed from the area. The inmate that was shot was transported off the yard by gurney, as were several other injured inmates.

It was another ninety minutes before the yard was cleared of inmates and ISU began processing the crime scenes. As per procedure, Belders and Riley surrendered their weapons, and they were replaced with different ones. Both were relieved from their positions and taken off of the main yard to the administration building for debriefing.

Riley walked down the hall to the debriefing room and opened the door and walked in. Belders was already sitting at a table. Riley went over to the table next to him and sat down. Riley eased back in his chair and said, "Now, about that truck."

Tommy King peered through the plastic doors on the food truck, trying to decide between a spinach salad or ordering a cheese burger. He opened the plastic door and reached into the shelves and retrieved a salad. He selected a couple of ranch dressing packets from a container. His beverage choice was unsweetened iced tea. He stood in line waiting to pay for his selections.

Sergeant Philips was coming from the parking lot and came around the food truck and saw King. "Hey, Lieutenant, didn't bring a lunch today?" he asked.

King shook his head aimlessly and responded, "I made it this morning, but my daughter asked me about her game this weekend and if I was going." He paused. "Anyway, we got to talking about what time and where, and we had a bonding moment about the game. But when we finished talking, I neglected to bond with my lunch and left it on the counter."

King noticed Philips had his lunch box in hand. "I see you have yours. Wanna trade?"

Philips said, "Let me think about that." He looked at the lieutenant's items. "Naw, I'll take my ravioli leftovers," he said laughing.

King nodded and said in a disappointing tone, "Thanks a lot." He paid for his fare and turned to go back inside the institution.

Philips had waited for King said, "Okay, Lieu, I'll escort you back inside so nobody steals your lunch."

King smiled and said, chuckling, "There's more of a chance that someone takes your lunch than mine."

They walked up to the entrance building and went around the counter, stopping to show their containers and IDs to the officer behind the counter. The officer briefly inspected the containers and took each ID, looked at the picture, and turned them over and looked at the backside of the ID. The officer said, "Thanks, Lieu, Sarge." With that, he pushed a button behind the counter.

They stepped into the sally port and closed the door behind them. They looked up to the top of the tower to their right, and the gate in front of them slid open, and they walked through. They continued up a few stair steps and went through the double doors into the administration building.

They angled to the right of a large entry area and then straight down a hallway to a control room. They waited for the outgoing traffic to navigate another sally port. When it was clear, they stepped through the door and closed it. They took their IDs and pressed them against the glass of the control room. The officer inside checked each one, and the lock on the door snapped, and Philips pulled it open.

Finally, they were inside the institution, a licensed medical and mental care facility. There were two long hallways directly in front of them, one straight ahead and the other spanned left and right. They both took to the right. They walked about forty feet down the hall, and King stopped at a door. Philips said, "Okay, Leiu, thanks for the escort."

King responded, "Anytime. Bon appétit."

The lock on the door snapped, and King pulled it open. He went into the watch office and off to the right. He went over to the Watch Sergeant's desk, and Sergeant Jones unclipped a set of keys from her belt and gave them to King. She said, "Here's your keys, Lieu."

King said, "Thanks, Jones. Anything earth shaking happen while I was gone?"

Jones replied, "Nope. All quiet so far."

He said, "Good." He turned and walked a few paces to the right. He unlocked a door and went into what is decidedly the smallest Watch Commander's office in the state. He sat down at his desk and sat his substitute lunch on it. He eased back in his chair, contemplating his meal.

The phone rang. King picked it up and stated, "Watch Commander King."

"Hi, lieutenant, this is Maloney."

King was taken aback. "Well, Jan Maloney, what would the Chief Deputy want with a lowly Watch Commander?"

"Well"—Jan paused—"I'm totally confused."

King pressed for a reason. "Okay, how can I clarify the confusion?"

"I'm not sure. I just got off the phone with the Deputy Director of Parole, Carson," Jan stated.

"This doesn't sound too good to start with," King said. "No, it's not," Jan said.

"Okay, you've got my attention." King took a slow breath.

"It seems that you have a civilian incarcerated in your institution," she asserted. "His name is Paul David Richards, K94682, in M-306."

King signed on in the computer and pulled up his information. "Okay, I see his file. Picked up as a PAL three weeks ago at Camp Pendleton and made his way to here. Okay, I'll bite. What's the story?"

Maloney continued, "It seems that he was on a bus that arrived at Camp Pendleton, where the guard at the gate ran his name and got a hit on him as a Parolee-At-Large from San Diego."

King was perplexed. "Okay, I follow so far, but what's the problem?"

"Ventura parole picked up a Parolee-At-Large yesterday, and he was positively identified as Paul David Richards, K94682."

King was trying to absorb the information and pressed for more. "So…who do I have here?"

"You also have Paul David Richards, a civilian. His family has been looking for him for the three weeks. It seems he got on the wrong bus in San Diego and arrived at Camp Pendleton," Maloney stated.

King was trying to filter through his thoughts. He said, "Okay, I gotta get MY Richards out of here and back home." He continued, "I need a contact number for his family."

Maloney said, "I just sent you the information."

"Thanks, Jan. I'll get him out ASAP," he said.

Maloney said, "Okay, call me when you have him safely secured." King said, "Will do," and hung up.

He sat for a moment in deep thought, wondering what HIS Richards has been going through.

*****

When Paul's mom and dad put him on the bus, they put his ID, medication, and appointment papers in a small nylon fanny pack and snapped it on him.

He was going to his aunt's house to start a treatment program. Paul was moderately mentally impaired, and the program was to enable him to better cope with daily life of a twenty-eight-year old. His parents had no vehicle and little funds to afford the program, but his aunt said she would get him into the program, and he could stay with her. They waved goodbye to their son as he left for the one-hour bus trip.

The bus left the depot and had traveled about half a mile. Paul was watching the cars along the streets and taking in the new sights. Suddenly, the bus began jerking, and the driver slowed down pulled over to the side of the road. The engine had died. The driver restarted the bus and turned the corner and headed back to the depot. He told his passengers that he was going back to the depot to get a different bus.

When he got back to the depot, the driver had the passengers get off and wait in a room while another bus was prepared. Paul got off with the other passengers and became a little stressed. He waited with the others for several minutes and felt the need to use the restroom. He asked someone where the restroom was and went in.

He unsnapped the fanny pack while he used the facilities. When he finished, he forgot to put the fanny pack back on and left it in the stall. He went back outside and became disoriented. He went over to a different area and stood with other people waiting to get on a bus. When he went up the steps, the driver asked where he was going. Paul reached for his fanny pack and became distressed and began to sob. He told the driver he had lost his fanny pack with the papers in it.

The driver asked where he was going. Paul became upset and said he couldn't remember exactly. The driver asked if he was going to Camp Pendleton. Paul recalled that he was going to some kind of center and that it could be a camp. The driver said that it was okay and to get on.

Paul's aunt was told the bus Paul was on would be late. She was relieved to see the bus finally arrive. She waited for Paul to get off. When he didn't, she called Paul's parents.

Paul's bus ride was longer than he had expected. He was missing his medication pills and was feeling noxious. When the bus stopped, he got off with the rest of the passengers. He stood around for several minutes, expecting to see his aunt. He noticed the guard shack and walked over to it.

A soldier stepped out of the building and met Paul. "Can I help you, sir?" he asked.

Paul said, "I don't feel too good. I lost my papers and medication. I need to call my aunt."

The soldier assessed Paul's actions fairly accurately as somewhat impaired and needing help. "Okay, sir. I'm Corporal Pierce. I'll try to get you some help. What's your name?"

Paul replied, "Paul."

Pierce smiled and said, "Okay, Paul, what's your full name?" Paul replied, "Paul David Richards."

Pierce told Paul to wait where he was. He stepped into his station and called his CO and told him about Paul. The CO directed Pierce to call dispatch, which he did. The dispatcher asked for his name.

After a few minutes he came back on the line. "Did you say Paul David Richards?" the voice asked.

"Yes, sir," Pierce replied.

"Okay, listen. Keep him there. A records search came back that he is a Parolee-At-Large from San Diego."

Pierce shook his head and said, "Sir, I don't think this is that Richards."

"Ask him where he is from."

Pierce stuck his head out of the door and asked Paul, "Sir, where are you from?"

Paul said, "I'm from San Diego, and I want to go back."

Pierce relayed the words to the dispatcher. The dispatcher said, "That's a match. Keep him there. I'll call San Diego Parole Office."

Pierce said, "Yes, sir."

The dispatcher contacted the parole office and told them they had a PAL. Parole normally picked up a PAL, but they said their agents were in a dragnet, and the best they could do for now was to have the county sheriff to pick him up.

As Paul waited, he became more stressed and incoherent. By the time deputies had arrived, Paul was swaying back and forth. Deputies Wyke and Perry cautiously approached Paul, noticing Paul's agitated state. Wyke asked Paul, "What's your name?"

Paul sort of mumbled, "Paul Richards." Wyke asked, "Do you have any ID?"

Paul became more agitated. He finally said, "No, I lost my papers and medication. I need to find my aunt."

Wyke asked Paul, "Are you Paul David Richards from San Diego?"

Paul said, "Yes."

Wyke told Paul, "Okay, San Diego Parole said you absconded, and we are to take you into custody."

Paul said, "What do you mean?"

Wyke said, "You broke parole, and you have to go back to prison."

Paul became anxious, "Nooooo, I don't want to go there. I want to find my aunt, and she'll take me to a home to get help."

Wyke had seen mentally impaired people before, but since he was supposed to be a wanted parolee, he had to take Paul to the county jail. Wyke decided not to place Paul in handcuffs, although protocol dictated it. He led Paul to his cruiser and said, "Richards, I'd like you to come with me so I can get you some help, okay?"

Paul was mumbling something unintelligible.

Wyke scanned Paul's clothing, looking for suspicious bulges that might be contraband or worse, a weapon. Wyke opened the car door, and as he helped Paul into the back seat, he quickly and surreptitiously patted him down and put his seatbelt on.

While they drove to the jail, Wyke contacted his supervisor on the radio. He related that Richards was relapsing from lack of medication and thought he should be evaluated. The supervisor agreed and said he would alert medical.

Paul's next stop was county jail. Wyke and Perry walked Paul up to the intake area and told Intake Deputy Frantz that Paul was said to be a PAL. Frantz studied Paul and said, "A PAL and no handcuffs?"

Perry said, "This guy may be a parolee, but sure doesn't act like one."

Wyke added, "The sarge said medical should check him out." Having no identification, Frantz gave Paul a temporary ID.

Frantz told Wyke, "Put him in holding 2."

Wyke led Paul over to a cell door and said to Paul, "Richards, will you wait in here until the doctor comes?"

Paul nodded, and Wyke opened the door and led Paul over to a bed. Wyke closed the door and locked it.

About an hour had gone by and the psychiatrist Dr. Ferrell looked into Paul's cell through the window. Paul was standing, facing the wall with his head against it, mumbling to himself. Ferrell opened the door and went in. He spoke to Paul, "Hello, Mr. Richards. I'm Dr. Ferrell. How are you?"

Paul looked at Ferrell and shook his head.

"Paul, are you taking any medication?" Ferrell asked. Paul said, "Yes, but I lost it."

The doctor asked him, "Do you know what medication you've been taking?"

Paul studied for a while and said, "I think it was Thorazine."

"Okay. Do you know where you are?" Ferrell asked.

"My aunt was going to meet me and take me somewhere to get some help."

"Okay, but do you know where you are?" he asked again. Paul said, "No."

"You are in the county jail."

"Noooo, why am I here?" Paul was noticeably upset. "You were picked up for violating your parole."

Paul asked, "What's that mean?"

Ferrell said, "The information I have is that you, Paul David Richards, were in prison, and when you were let out of prison, you failed to contact your Parole Agent."

Paul waved his arms and hands, saying, "Nooooo, I didn't go to prison. That isn't me." Paul raised his voice. "I'm not who you think I am."

Farrell tried to deescalate the tension and spoke in a soft tone, "Okay, Paul, we'll get you some help."

Ferrell left the cell. He seemed convinced that Paul was showing symptoms of schizophrenia and prescribed Thorazine for Paul.

The next morning, after taking his medication, Paul's condition had somewhat stabilized. Paul was still in the cell when a different psyche came back see him.

The psyche asked Paul, "How do you feel today?"

Paul looked at the doctor and said, "I'm not who you think I am."

The doctor asked, "Okay, Paul then who are you?"

"I'm Paul David Richards," he replied.

The doctor said calmly, "Paul, that's who I think you are." Paul said, "But I'm not who you think I am."

The doctor said, "Then are you someone else also?"

Paul, visibly irritated, replied, "No, I'm Paul Richards, but I'm not who you think I am."

The doctor asked, "Is the medication you're taking helping?" Paul said, "Yes, but I'm not who you think I am."

The psyche nodded and left.

Every chance Paul got, he told most everyone he talked to, "I'm not who you think I am."

The deputies in his unit had good laughs at Paul's expense. The county jail officials contacted the local parole and told them that

Richards was possibly suffering from schizophrenia. Parole failed check the file on Parolee Richards to match Paul with his information. Parole said that a bus would pick him up on the next trip.

Three days later, a bus finally arrived and transported him to CIM in Chino. When he arrived at Chino reception, he was photographed, fingerprinted, and issued a new ID with "Paul David Richards, K94682." It was unbelievable how Paul fell through the cracks in the system. He told the officer putting him in a holding cell, "I'm not who you think I am."

He stayed at Chino for one week, still expressing to anyone who would listen, "I'm not who you think I am."

Eventually, he was transferred to DVI in Tracy, where he continued to express to everyone, "I'm not who you think I am."

A psyche evaluation also assessed Paul as schizophrenic and prescribed Thorazine. The medication helped Paul clear his mind somewhat, but he continued to express, "I'm not who you think I am."

That ongoing statement served only to reinforce a schizophrenic diagnosis. He spent ten days at DVI, and since Paul was on Thorazine, it seemed logical that he should be transferred to a medical/mental facility, and that was his next destination: California Medical Facility.

In Paul's mind, his reasoning was sound, but no one would listen to him. Regardless of how many times he would say, "I'm not who you think I am," no one understood what he was trying to say. His mental health diagnosis and Thorazine regiment landed him in a single-cell fishbowl-style unit M-3—or as it is called, Mary 3. In there, Paul devolved into a deeply depressed soul with little hope and no care for physical cleanliness.

Each time he was approached, Paul would repeat his mantra, "I'm not who you think I am."

*****

Lieutenant King dialed the phone for M-3 unit sergeant. "Program 3, Sergeant Philips."

"Philips, King."

"No, Tommy, I'm not trading lunches with you," Philips said, laughing.

King looked at the untouched lunch on his desk, thinking it would be molded before he got to it. "Yeah, probably won't get to eat it anyway. You had yours?"

"Yep, all gone. Too late," Philips said.

"That's good, but what I've got to tell you would certainly interfere with your digestion," King stated.

"How's that, Lieu?"

"You have a Richards in M-306," King stated.

"Oh, yeah, Mr. 'I'm not who you think I am,'" Philips quipped. King said, "Well, he's NOT who you think he is."

Philips laughed, "Okay, Lieu, you been sniffing something?"

"After the call I just got from the Chief Deputy, we all may need to sniff something."

Philips noted the serious tone in King's voice. "Okay, what's up?"

King said, "The real Paul David Richards, K94682, was picked up yesterday by Ventura Parole, positive ID."

"So who do I have in M-306?" Philips asked. "You have Paul David Richards, a civilian."

Philips paused for a moment processing. "Wow, holy shit."

King continued, "You need to get him out of the cell and bring him to me. Keep him safe."

Philips said, "You got it, Lieu. On my way."

Philips hung up and called M-3 unit. After several rings, there came an answer. "Mary 3, Perez."

"Perez, Philips. I need you to get Richards in 306 out and put him in your office. Do not hurt him in anyway by any means."

Perez was intrigued by the statement. "Okay, Sarge. What's up?"

Philips said, "I'll explain when I get there. Again, no harm to him at all, got it?"

Perez said, "10-4, Sarge."

Philips left his office in a flash and negotiated the two sets of stairs to the third floor. He made his way to the far end of the third floor to M-3. He took his set of keys and opened the door and locked it behind him. He saw Officer Clark down the walk way and headed straight for him. The door to 306 was open, and Perez was partway inside. He was talking to Richards. "Richards, can you please come out of the cell?"

Perez was bent down, looking under the bunk where Richards was ensconced. The smell in the cell was atrociously unbearable from sweat and feces. Richards replied, "No, I'm not coming out. I'm not who you think I am."

Sergeant Philips took a turn. "Richards, this is Sergeant Philips.

I would like you to come out of the cell."

Richard's response was, "No, I'm not who you think I am."

After two more tries to get him to come out, Philips called King on the radio. "Watch Commander, Sergeant Philips."

"Go ahead, Philips," was King's reply. "Can you 10-20 Mary 3 ASAP?"

"10-4. En route," King said.

Philips went down the hall and opened the unit door to wait for King. Within a minute, King was coming down the third floor hallway. Philips held the door, and King went in. "What's going on?" King asked.

Philips said, "He's refusing to come out."

King took a deep breath, and with that, he made his way to the cell. He stood at the door, shaking his head from the smell coming from the cell. He took a breath of fresh air and went in to the cell. Richards was still under the bunk. King said, "Richards, this is Lieutenant King. Can you come out? I'd like to talk to you."

Richards replied, "No, I'm not who you think I am."

King thought for a moment. He stepped up to the bunk and bent down. He saw Richards in a fetal position. King reached down and held out his hand and said, "Paul, I know who you are, and I've come to take you home."

Even through the darkness, King thought he could see a glimmer of hope in Paul's beleaguered eyes. Paul responded, "You're taking me home?"

King said, "Yes, Paul, you're going home."

Paul took King's hand and slowly egressed from his horrible experience. When Paul stood up, he hugged King, who cringed from the smell but not the hug." King said, "You're okay. You're safe. But, buddy, can you take a shower?"

Paul laughed. It was probably the first time Paul had smiled in months and surely his first laugh.

As it happened, Paul's family had frantically been searching for him since he didn't show up where his aunt was waiting at the bus depot. Fliers and contacts with hospitals, morgues, and police were fruitless. They were ecstatic over the news that Paul was coming home.

The Chief Deputy made arrangements for Paul to fly home. Paul was adamant that he wouldn't fly unless Lieutenant King went with him. He was the only one he trusted.

When King escorted Paul out of the institution, all normal protocols were suspended. There was no paperwork for staff to check, and no one questioned King or Paul when they went through all the security checkpoints. Lieutenant King and Paul had a first class trip flight to San Diego, and King met his eternally grateful family.

After all the missteps of various agencies and correctional staff, the Richards family was probably well compensated. But to Paul, "I Know Who You Are."

THE FISHBOWL

Officer Carson stepped out of his booth and checked the ID of the driver of the vehicle that had stopped at the entrance gate.

"What's up, Morton?" he said.

"Same stuff, another day," Morton replied.

Carson looked into the vehicles interior and nodded to Morton and said, "Have a good one."

"Thanks," Morton replied and continued toward the parking lot. He parked his car and got out and took off his windbreaker and put it on the seat. He stepped to the driver's side back door and opened it and retrieved his duty belt and put it around his waist. He got out his lunch bag and closed the car doors and pressed the lock button on his key fob.

As he walked toward the entrance building, he looked across the open field toward one of the observation booths situated on a raised berm serving as an option to a perimeter tower. He walked past the administration building and opened the door to the entrance building. There were a few staff talking to each other off to the far left side of the room.

He went over toward the counter and sat his lunch bag on it and opened it. He waited for the entrance officer, Parsons, to clear another staff and got out his ID. Parsons came over to Morton, checked his ID, and looked into his lunch bag to inspect it. "Where you at today?" Parsons asked.

"I'm in 513 today," Morton said as he closed and gathered his lunch bag. "Another day in the fishbowl."

Parsons smiled as Morton walked toward the exit door. Officer Johnson was waiting at the door and nodded to Morton and said, "Afternoon."

Morton replied, "Johnson, you get those swaps worked out?"

The door lock snapped open, and the two stepped through and closed the door. Johnson replied, "Yeah, all lined up. Can't wait to take the family to the Grand Canyon."

"Hope you guys have a fun time," Morton added.

They came to a split in the walkway, and Johnson stopped and said, "Okay, Morty, catch you later. Going over to Seg to work today," motioning to his left."

"Okay, Johnson, have fun over there," Morton said, smiling.

Morton continued to the next building and opened the door to the complex entrance building. He waved to the officer at a counter and walked to the exit door and waited for the officer to push a button behind the counter to unlock the door. When he heard the lock snap, he walked out and closed the door.

In front of Morton was an immense open yard, probably two hundred yards long and one hundred yards wide, that contained a running track to the right. He continued ahead on a wide pathway, meeting several staff. He continued until he got close to a yard complex building and went to the left and passed a couple of housing units and stopped at his destination.

The housing unit was a single building with a multitude of windows all around the unit. An officer in the unit saw Morton at the door and waited for her to unlock the door. Officer Collins opened the door, let Morton in, and relocked the door. "Afternoon, Sally," Morton said with a smile.

"Hey, Morty, welcome home," she said with a chuckle.

Inside the unit was an officer's station centered in the front half of the building. The officer's station itself offered a 360-degree view from inside and outside through plated glass windows. Morton scanned the inmates' activities in the unit and followed Collins into the office portion of the officer's station and then into a separate secure officers' area that Collins unlocked.

Morton put his lunch bag on a desk and asked, "Who am I relieving, Billings?"

"Yep. He's in the bathroom," Collins said as she walked out of the office.

Morton turned to set of clipboards hanging along the lower half of the windowed wall and took one off. He inspected the inmate movement sheet and placed it back on its hook. He sat down in a chair and opened up the Daily Activity Report book and read through the last pages and put it down.

He noticed Billings walking toward the office and stood up to greet him. "Billings, how's it going?"

"Great now that you're here," he said.

"Well, let's make it better. Give me your stuff and you're out. Deal?" Morton asked. "Deal."

Billings took off the radio, alarm, keys, and OC from his duty belt. Morton carefully took each item and inspected each item as he placed it on his duty belt. Billings said, "Nothing major going on. Just setting up laundry. Other than that, zip."

"That's good to hear," Morton said.

Billings picked up his lunch box and turned to walk out of the office. Morton followed him out of the office and closed the self-locking door behind him. They continued to the unit exit door, and Morton unlocked it and let Billings out.

Morton stepped outside and closed the door. He looked around the yard area between the other units and noted several inmates standing near the doors of the units. He saw Inmate Wilson and several other inmates walking quickly around the corner of another unit toward his unit. He turned toward the door and unlocked it and opened it. He started inside when Wilson called out to him. "Officer Morton, can you hold the door," she pleaded.

Morton stated. "Wilson, unlock is not until 1445."

"I know, but I want to catch the rest of my TV show."

"Wilson, you know I've got laundry set up, and it comes first before an 'in line.'"

Several other inmates came up and were standing around. "Yes, but Officer Billings always lets me in."

"Sorry, Wilson, but you'll have to wait another half hour till Collins and I can set the laundry bags up, then we can do an 'in line.'"

"Oh, Officer Morton, please let me in"—still pleading.

Morton smiled at the group of inmates opened the door and said, "No, you'll still have to wait a bit."

He stepped inside, and while closing the door, he heard some other inmates commenting, "Oh, wow," and other expletives.

He locked the door and walked over to several inmates sorting out laundry bags by room number. He greeted the inmates, "Afternoon, ladies."

A smattering of "Afternoon" and "Hi, CO," were delivered.

He continued down one of the hallways, visually noting each five person pod and its occupants. Each pod was walled halfway up with the upper potion open. He did the same for the other hallway and returned to the officer's station and stood next to Officer Collins. "I see Wilson is still 'trying' her best," Collins said.

"Yeah, mostly trying to make herself special," Morton chuffed. "She tries to get here before Billings leaves, but she should know her ploy doesn't work with us," Collins said, shaking her head.

Morton stated, "I saw on the movement sheet four new inmates."

"Yeah, I caught a glimpse of one in pod 3. Guess we'll orientate them after laundry gets done."

"Sounds like a plan."

The two went inside the officer's station, observing the laundry setup from their side of the "fishbowl." After a few moments, Morton stretched out his shoulders and turned to Collins. "Guess I'll take a tour of the unit."

Collins nodded her head, and he walked out of the officer's station and headed down one of the hallways, glancing from one pod to the other, taking note of the inmates and the bed areas of each one. Occasionally, he would step into a pod and search suspicious clothing, lockers, toilet, and shower areas for contraband. He was mindful of being cautious in his intrusions so as not to appear voyeuristic in the female environment.

Since his academy days, Morton has taken to heart some of the caveats of working in a woman's joint. An inmate is an inmate, male or female. Inmates generally do what you tell them to do and want consistency and structure. Respect inmates as a person, not confusing that with their crime. Your job is to supervise their behavior, set an example, and keep them safe. You should realize that you are not there to punish them. Their punishment is being separated from society, thereby keeping society safe.

There are differences in dealing with female inmates aside from the obvious physiological differences and hygiene needs. They tend to be more pragmatic and ask why. Although being emotional is not unique to female inmates, they do have more than their share of underlying psychological aspects. They have more concerns about their family on the outside. The care of their children usually falls to their mothers, sisters, or grandmother. Their corresponding male involvement is usually non-existent. They have decisively much less visitation than the male inmates. They are generally forgotten by all but family. They have a tendency to develop a "family structure" with other inmates, creating a mother, sister, and/or husband relationships. The pitfall for staff, male or female, is not seeing them as inmates but rather equate them as a mother, sister, or lover.

Four unit inmate workers were busy near the TV area, sorting laundry bags by pod and bed number. Inmates place the clothing items in the bags that they want washed, and then the bags are sent to the laundry facility, washed, and returned to the unit.

Inmate Parker came over to Collins and said, "Officer Collins, we're done sorting. You want us to put them on the beds now?"

Collins replied, "Sure, Parker. That would be great. Thanks."

Parker walked back to the other workers and said, "Let's go, girls."

In rather organized fashion, the crew began grabbing groups of bags and scurried down the various hallways, placed the bags on matching bed numbers, and returned for another group of bags. When the last group of bags disappeared, Parker came back to Collins. "Miss Collins, we're done," she reported.

Collins replied, "Okay, you gals are good to go. Thanks."

Parker nodded and went back to the other workers, nodded to them, and they separated to various parts of the unit. Collins saw Morton at the desk in the office and went over to him and said, "Okay, laundry bags are out."

Morton nodded and feigned disappointment. "I guess that means 'I' have to make a trip to the door and let the kids in."

Collins smiled. "Well, you need to make amends for locking Wilson outside."

Morton half laughed as said, "Thanks."

He looked through the windows at the gaggle standing outside the unit entrance door. He walked past Collins and out of the officer's station. As he approached the door, he reached for his keys. The inmates saw him approaching. They gathered up shirts and other items, and Morton chuckled internally. He got a mind-flash that likened the inmates' excitement to that of a pet's excitement seeing their master coming to the door. He shook off the vision and unlocked the door and stepped outside. "Okay, ladies. Thank you for your patience. You may enter," he said, smiling.

As the fifteen or so inmates came in, a few "Thanks, CO,"

"Afternoon," and head-nods were offered. Morton at times would stop an inmate and do a pat down search of an inmate or items they were carrying. He scanned the area, looking for stragglers. He saw none and walked back inside and locked the door.

He began to make another tour of the unit. He veered off to his right toward the TV viewing area. Several inmates had settled into the chairs and padded couch style benches, watching with their earphones plugged into outputs tuned to one of the TV monitors mounted on the wall. He went past the second TV area and settled momentarily by the dayroom area with various tables and couches where inmates would read, play games, and socialize. He glanced out of a window and saw some staff and inmates walking in the areas between the units. He continued around the dayroom area back to the officer's station where Collins stood, talking to inmate Parker. He went over and picked up the inmate roster and waited until they finished talking.

Parker left, and he stepped over to Collins and asked, "You ready to talk to the newbies?"

"Yep," she replied. "I just sent Parker to collect them and have them meet us in the dayroom."

"Okay," he said as he looked at the inmate roster. As read the roster he continued, "Looks like three are new arrivals, and Rios just got kicked out of Seg."

Collins nodded. "Yeah, Rios did a week in Seg for assaulting an inmate over property. I was gonna pull the 832 but thought I'd wait till we talk to her."

"Yep, let's hear her story first," Morton agreed. "Let's go check out their flimsies," Collins said.

Morton followed her into the office. The "flimsy files" are abbreviated versions of an inmate's crime and history. Both sat down at a desk and shared reading the inmate files for several minutes. Both looked up often to scan the inmate activity from their side of the fishbowl. Morton shook his head as he read. "You know…I'd like to see the complete abstract on Barber. I think she got a raw deal. But I guess they all have a story, and we don't have the time to go through every case."

Collins added, "Yeah, I hate to read about some of the things inmates have done and those that seem to have been wronged."

Morton closed a file and sat looking out at the unit. Collins closed her last file and sat, digesting the information. "I'm ready. You?"

Morton nodded and stood up. Collins stood also, and they left the office and locked the both doors of the officer's station. They made their way to the dayroom area where the new inmates were sitting.

Collins deliberately looked at each inmate one after the other. "Do you all speak and understand English?"

They all nodded, and a couple said yes.

She began. "Okay, ladies, welcome to 513. I'm Officer Collins, and this is Officer Morton. We're usually here together on third watch four days a week, and one of us is here two of the other days. We try to run this unit as smooth as possible. And with your cooperation, all of us can get through our day without incidents. Morton and I will treat you with respect so long as you treat us and those in the unit with respect." She turned to Morton for his turn.

Morton started his oratory. "We have a nice unit here. You can ask around this unit and other units. Most everyone would rather live in this unit. We, and I personally, will respect you privacy as a woman as much as possible, but I will do my job. Except while showering, you will wear appropriate tops, pants or gowns, and undergarments at all times, even while sleeping. Don't expose yourself to anyone. I will search your property and your person with dignity, consideration, and professionalism. I have a sense of humor, and sometimes, I can go a little too far, and I've been called on it. Rest assured that I, we"—pointing to Collins—"will not appreciated being played. We've worked together long enough to know each other's habits, good and bad."

He smiled at Collins. He continued, "If you have problems in the unit, we will try to help if we can. We are not counselors, but we feel that knowing what you're about helps us deal with situations that may come up. If you have personal issues with hygiene or with family, we'll try to help or find someone who can."

Collins took another turn. She looked at the inmates and said, "Each of you show me your ID."

She took each ID, looked at it, and passed it to Morton, who looked at each one and handed them back to Collins. She called each name. "Barber, Walters, and Brascia, you're first termers and new to our institution. You will need some time to adjust to prison life." She paused. "I can't tell you who you should associate with, but I can tell you that if it doesn't feel right to do something, it's probably not."

She turned to Rios. "Rios, we see you came from Ad Seg. We have some information about what happened, but here, you have a clean slate. If you want to tell us about it, we'll listen."

Morton picked up the discourse. "When you come up to our office, stand and wait for us to address you, as we may be busy. If you want to know about our general program here, ask Parker, the inmate that asked you to meet us. If you have questions now, we'll answer. Or if you want to catch us individually later, we're okay with that too."

Morton paused for any response. The group seemed to have been listening attentively. There were some nodding and positive facial expressions from the group. Collins broke the silence. "Okay, ladies, that's all we have for now. It's getting close to count time, and then we have chow, so…thanks for listening."

Inmates Walters and Barber said, "Thank you," and the other two nodded.

Collins and Morton headed for the officer's station.

Collins and Morton busied themselves by filling out the DAR (Daily Activity Report) and reading some inmate mail until count time was announced on the radio. Collins reached over to a light switch on the wall and turned on the red count lights in the hallways. Morton went to the desk and keyed up the unit microphone. "Okay, ladies, it's count time, count time. This is a standing count." Collins and Morton each picked up a clipboard and placed a piece of paper on the clipboards. They waited momentarily for a few inmates to scurry back to their living quarters. "You ready partner?" Collins asked.

Morton replied, "Lead the way, madam."

They slowly walked down to the end of one of the hallways and turned around, each one methodically counting each inmate as they stood by their bed. When they came back to the front of the hallway, they stopped and compared their counts of the inmates. Their counts agreed. They split up, and each walked around the officer's station to ensure that no inmates had slipped around to avoid the count or doubled back to cause a miscount. They rejoined at the start of the next hallway and started their count there and continued the same count process.

As they approached the pod that Inmate Wilson was assigned to, she pulled open the shower door, leaned out, partially exposed her upper body, and said, "I'm here, Miss Collins."

Collins and Morton both saw her state of undress. They looked at each other and shook their heads in distaste. They continued their count till the end of the hallway. There they compared their counts, and they were the same total. (Inmates are aware they are not to leave their bed area until count is cleared.)

They walked back to the office, and Collins filled out a count slip. She picked up the phone and dialed a number. Momentarily, she spoke, "Collins in 513 with count." She paused. "92," she stated.

"Thank you," she said and hung up the phone.

Morton picked up the count slip and said, "I'll put this out." He walked over to the entrance door, opened it, stepped out,

and put the count slip in a narrow slot in a small box on the side of the door, then came back in and locked the door. He proceeded back to the office and sat down at the desk with Collins. Morton spoke. "Wilson was over the line with her shower stunt. I'll have to talk to her about it and maybe give her a write-up."

Collins nodded her head and said, "I got your back on that. She is pushing the envelope."

Morton and Collins were reading more inmate mail when the radio announced that the institutional count was clear. Collins turned off the red count lights. Morton reached for the unit microphone and announced, "Count is clear."

Immediately, inmates began scurrying around the unit, preparing to go to chow. Collins noticed an officer outside the unit door, taking the count slip out of the box. After several minutes, the radio announced that units could release their inmates to go to chow. Collins keyed the unit microphone and announced, "Chow."

Morton and Collins stood up and walked together out of the office, locking the doors behind them. They went over to the unit door, and Collins unlocked it and opened it wide. They stood inside the unit and looked over each inmate to ensure appropriated attire and checked each ID the inmate showed as they exited.

After several minutes, the line disappeared, and Collins closed and locked the door. She and Morton walked down each hallway, checking the unit for any inmates that didn't go to eat. Morton saw

Inmate Foster sitting on her bunk, reading a book. Morton went over to her and asked, "Foster, not going to chow?"

"Naw, not really hungry. I have some canteen stuff to snack on if I get hungry," she said.

Morton looked at her face, hands, and arms for any cuts, bruises, or other trauma that might indicate injury. Occasionally, an inmate could be threatened or intimidated into not leaving the unit.

Morton continued to the end of the hallway and saw no other inmates. He turned around and came back to the dayroom area and waited for Collins. Eventually, she joined Morton. "Foster didn't go to chow. She seemed okay," Morton stated.

"Olsen and Marberry are still here also," she countered. "Shall we eat now or later?" Morton asked.

"Well, as sure as we don't eat, something could go down, and we may not get to eat," Collins stated.

"Yep, could happen," he agreed.

They returned back to the office and gathered their lunch bags and began to eat. As a routine, they would eat some of their lunch and save a little for later. Inmates returning from chow usually cut their mealtime short as a rule.

They sat eating and talking for about ten more minutes when they noticed inmates returning to the unit. Morton put his lunch away and said, "I'll get the door. You can finish your sandwich."

Collins nodded. Morton stood up and went to the entrance door and unlocked and opened it. Soon, the unit was abuzz with inmates entering and moving about. Collins put the rest of her lunch away and left the station, locking the doors. She watched the inmate activity and kept an eye on Morton.

Each inmate showed their ID to Morton as they entered. Occasionally, he would stop the inmates coming in and search a bag an inmate had or pat down the inmate. The flow of inmates finally stopped, and Morton waited a moment for latecomers then closed and locked the door. He walked back to the officer's station and joined Collins.

Several inmate workers began sweeping and wiping furniture and tables in the unit. The eight to twenty cents an hour allowed an inmate worker to buy items at the canteen instead of waiting for a package of items from a catalogue.

Morton and Collins stood in the officer's station, again watching the inmates from their side of the fishbowl. The inmates' activities and grouping verified that most people are creatures of habit. Watching the same TV shows, playing the same table games, and hanging out with the same group.

Generally, female inmates don't have a close bond as a gang, not that there aren't alliances to street or prison gangs, but they are not usually as structured as male inmates. They rarely have one inmate that controls an institution or yard as a shot caller. Most of the violence vested in female prisons is usually for personal reasons, and an attack often is to disfigure, an assault on their vanity.

Morton looked at Collins and said, "Guess it's time to talk to Wilson."

Collins half smiled and said, "I'll wait by the dayroom and come back when she comes up." He went over to the unit microphone. "Inmate Wilson, D-4, report to the officer's station."

He walked over to the door and sat down on a stool just inside the officer's station. After a few minutes, Collins saw Inmate Wilson walking up to Morton, and she timed her arrival with Wilson's and stood behind her. Wilson was smiling at Morton, leaned toward him, and said in a sweet voice, "Officer Morton, did you want to see me?"

Morton noticed her lean toward him, allowing her top to open up excessively, exposing her bra-less cleavage. Morton said sternly, "Wilson, you know you're to wear undergarments."

Wilson said, "Well, you didn't seem to mind when you were doing the count."

"Well, you're wrong," he said.

Collins chimed in from behind. "Yes, you are."

Wilson was surprised by Collins. Morton said, "Get dressed properly and come back up."

Wilson turned and walked back toward her pod. Morton and Collins shook their heads and smiled. Collins stated, "She IS pushing it."

Morton nodded and said, "Yep."

They both waited in the officer's station, reading mail until Wilson returned. After a few minutes later, Wilson came back to the office. Morton began, "Wilson, I shouldn't have to restate the rules and our expectations of behavior. You've been in this unit for several months."

Wilson stood stoically, listening.

Morton continued, "Director's rules 3004, 3005, and 3007 deal with rights and respect, conduct, and sexual behavior, and you are accountable to those rules just as I am. I choose to adhere to those rules to show respect to you, other inmates, and"—turning to Collins—"and staff."

He continued, "You seem to want to challenge my professionalism by disrespecting me—actually, us"—nodding to Collins—"by bending or violating those rules.

He paused.

"We try to run a safe and easy running unit, and it is put at risk when the lines are crossed by either inmates or staff."

He paused again.

"I believe that being consistent is an important element in dealing with people. We are all generally creatures of habit, but if I came to work pleasant and happy one day and the next day I came in grumpy and snapped at you, you wouldn't know which person I'd be from day to day. That would probably make you uncomfortable every day." Again, he paused.

"I understand that you may want to be liked by others or specifically me. Certainly, being human, I may have tendencies to have favorites, but I cannot maintain a professional standard if I favor one person over another, and I cannot run a successful and safe unit on that basis."

He paused for a final time.

"So bottom line, dress appropriately and don't try to sweet talk me or try to curry favor with me. I will give you respect, so respect me, and we will both make the best of each day for everyone."

Wilson seemed somewhat pensive. He waited for her reaction. Wilson finally responded. "Okay, Officer Morton. I get it." She paused. "Am I getting a write-up?"

Morton dropped one brow. "Not at this time. I'll chalk this up as miscommunication. Is that okay? Are we good?"

Wilson said, "Yeah, we're good." Morton said, "Okay."

He turned to Collins. "Collins, you got anything for her?" Collins said, "Nope. Think you said it all."

Wilson turned around and left. Morton took a noticeable breath. Collins watched him for a moment and said, "I didn't know if she was going to go to sleep on you or cry, but I always enjoy your diatribes." She smiled and shook her head.

Morton chuckled. "Glad you enjoyed it," he said. "Well, gonna make some rounds." He turned and ambled off toward the dayroom. Collins locked the door and went in the opposite direction.

They toured the housing unit, interacting with the patrons.

Morton was talking to some inmates in the dayroom area, and Collins was coming out of one of the hallways toward the office when some quick movements on the yard area outside of the unit caught her eye. She ran around the office to get a better view. Morton noticed her running and assessed her concern. She was looking out the window behind Morton. He spun around and saw two inmates grabbing and hitting each other. He saw an officer running toward them. Collins keyed up her radio and announced, "Control, Officer Collins. I have a Code 3. Inmates fighting in the yard on the west side of 513. Officer responding."

Morton yelled to the inmates in the unit, "Get down. Everybody, down."

The inmates began to comply. Collins yelled to Morton, "I'm going, you got the unit."

Morton yelled, "Okay, go!"

The radio crackled, "Control copies. Yard 5 Sergeant, do you copy?"

"This is 5 Sergeant. I copy."

Collins ran to the exit door and unlocked and opened it. Morton arrived at the door right behind her. He said, "I got the door."

She ran out the door, and Morton closed and locked it. He followed Collins's flight from inside the fishbowl.

She ran around the side of the building toward the incident. She saw the other officer aiming a canister of OC at the inmates and telling them to stop and get down on the ground. Collins saw one of the inmates holding something in her right hand and swinging it at the other inmate.

As she got closer, the other officer sprayed at the faces of the inmates. Collins noted that one of the inmates had red marks on her face and arms that appeared to be cuts. Collins saw the inmate with the weapon turn her back toward Collins and ran into her back and shoulder area with her own arm and shoulder knocking that inmate into the other inmate, and both inmates fell to the ground. The other officer quickly put her OC away and put her knee on the back of one of the inmates on the ground to keep her down.

The other inmate that Collins had run into was starting to get up again. She still had the weapon in her hand. Collins pulled out her baton and snapped it to its full extension and told the inmate to stop and get down. The inmate didn't immediately comply, and Collins struck the inmate's right arm with the baton. The inmate yelled and fell back down. Two additional responding officers arrived at the scene, and one assisted Collins in keeping that inmate on the ground. Collins put her baton away and pulled out her handcuffs. She put her cuffs on her inmate, and the other officers put the other inmate in restraints also.

Collins keyed up her radio, "Control, Officer Collins. Code 4.

No further response needed. Need a gurney and medical"

"Control copies. Watch Commander, Officer Collins advises Code 4. Break...medical and gurney needed on west side of unit 513."

"Medical en route."

Collins and responding officer Banta each put on latex gloves. They assisted the inmate to a standing position. Collins bent down and picked up the weapon used in the attack. It appeared to be a sharpened piece of flat metal about three inches in length with one end wrapped with cloth as a handle. They began to escort the inmate toward medical.

The inmate yelled at the other inmate, "I told you I'd get you, you fuckin' bitch."

They continued toward medical. The other two officers, Jones and Pierce, were surveying the cuts on their inmate while they put on gloves. There were two slashes on the left arm and one on the left cheek and one on the left side of the neck. The cuts were bleeding only slightly. Jones asked the inmate, "Can you walk?"

The inmate nodded.

Jones and Pierce helped the inmate up. Jones keyed up his radio, "Control, this is Officer Jones, 10-22 the gurney and medical. Inmate is ambulatory and will be escorted to medical."

Control responded, "10-4, Jones. Medical, do you copy?"

"This is medical. I copy. 10-22 our response."

"Control to all units, resume normal movement."

Back in the fishbowl, Officer Morton was watching the incident unfold. He walked over to the office area, unlocked the door, and keyed up the unit microphone. "Okay, ladies, all clear."

Morton stood in the office, watching the inmates moving about. Since he was alone in the unit, he stayed semisafe, being visible to those outside the unit.

About fifteen minutes later, he saw Officer Collins come back into the unit. She walked into the office, and Morton had a grin on his face. He extended his fist out for a fist bump. Collins had a quizzical look on her face as she bumped his fist. Morton said, "That was quite a block you put on the inmate out there you linebacker you."

Collins responded, "Just saw the opening and took it. Guess it was pretty awesome. You get it on video?"

Morton exclaimed, "Burned into my mind forever."

They laughed. They stood in the glassed in officer's station, looking out of their side of the fishbowl. The inmates peered back at them from their side. As much as there is to see from either side, you may sometimes realize that your fishbowl may be inside of yet another fishbowl.

Bronson walked past the dialysis unit of the FSS central medical complex on his way to B Complex. The overhangs made the complex look more like storefronts of a high-end, open air outlet mall than a prison. He greeted and nodded to several medical and custody staff and approached AB Complex entrance. The gate opened, and he walked in, and the gate closed. He showed his ID to the officer at the counter. "Good morning, John," the officer said.

Bronson responded, "Hey, Culp, what's up?"

"Nada," was his response as he reached and pushed a button to open the exit gate.

Bronson turned and headed down to the B Complex and turned down the walkway. He went past Bravo units 1, 2, 3 and arrived at his unit, B4 B-side, Bravo 4 Bravo. He waited for the officer to unlock the door. Officer Patel opened the door, and Bronson stepped in. "Mornin', Carl," Bronson said.

"Hey, John," was the reply.

Bronson walked down to the open air officer's station in the center of the unit and put his lunch box under the counter. He waved his head to Officer Patrick at the other end of the station. Patrick came over to Bronson and said, "You my relief, floor 3?"

"Yep, that's me," Bronson replied.

"That's cool," he said, removing each piece of equipment and handing each one to Bronson: cuffs, baton, PAD alarm, OC, and key group.

Bronson put each piece of equipment on his duty belt. Bronson said, "Okay, ready to go?"

"Yeah. Thanks for the early relief." Bronson nodded. "No problem."

They both went to the unit door, and Bronson let him out. Bronson saw Officer Macias coming toward the unit and waited for him. Macias got to the door and said, "Good morning, John," and extended his fist for a fist bump, which was accepted.

Bronson closed the door, and they walked together to the officer's station.

Bronson went over to the computer, sat down, and logged on. He searched the inmate movement page and the Daily Activity Report. After a few minutes, he logged off.

He opened up the 114 folder to check Ad Seg inmate activity for anything unusual. This 114 folder contains documentation of when an Ad Seg inmate showers, is fed, goes to the yard, leaves the unit and returns, and even if they are awake during the time the officer checks on them during their shift. This is mandated by ongoing court order.

Administratively segregated (Ad Seg) inmates are placed in separate areas of an institution when they present a safety and security risk to the institution. Often, their placement in Ad Seg is due to assaulting someone or the victim of assault. Other reasons may include possession of weapons, drugs, or other dangerous contraband—any serious violation of <u>Title 15, Director's Rules</u>. Ad Seg is akin to the jail within the prison. They are generally considered to be subject to maximum security status with even less freedom of movement and privileges than that of general population (GP) inmates. Their movement outside of cells require placement in restraints and escort by staff.

Bronson finished reading the 114 Ad Seg folder and put the folder back. Bronson heard a radio transmission come from Macias's radio. "Bravo 4 Bravo, chow on your back door."

Patel keyed his radio, "4 Bravo copies." Patel headed toward the back of the unit and opened the door.

Bronson heard some noise at far end of the unit. He saw the food carts coming through the door. Two inmate workers were being escorted in by kitchen staff. They rolled the cooler/cooker carts over to the wall and plugged them in. Officer Patel watched the process and counted the paper trays of food and beverages inside when they finished. Verifying the needed count, he followed the kitchen workers to the exit door, opened it, and let them out.

Macias was toward the end of the counter, putting on a PPE coverall, pulling it up, stopping halfway to the waist. Patel joined him. Bronson walked over to him and pulled out a PPE out of the cupboard and put it on, also stopping at the waist. The crew, as a matter of course, chose to wear PPEs. Situations can get out of control quickly, and although it only take a minute to put them on, that minute can be critical.

Bronson finished donning his PPE and walked over to cell 101 and saw Inmate Ross sitting on his bunk. He continued down the single level tier, noting each inmate's activity and if there was a "MAX" sign above the door. He got to the end at cell 116 and went across to the other side of the tier and came back up the tier, looking into each of the other cells, and finished at cell 133. He walked back over to the officer's station and stood next to Officer Macias. Bronson asked, "What'd you do on your RDOs?"

Macias half smiled and said, "Two days off are never enough. But it cost me some coin. Had to get new tires for the beast."

Bronson laughed. "Keep your damn foot out of the carburetor and you wouldn't burn the rubber off."

Macias shrugged his shoulders, "Yeah, but 485 horses gotta eat."

"How much hay did they eat?" Bronson countered.

"Eighteen bills worth," Macias said, dropping his head down.

"Damn," Bronson said. "There goes the OT up in smoke."

Officer Patel walked over and caught the last part of the conversation. "What cost eighteen bills?"

"Tires for dude's ride," Bronson replied.

Patel said, smirking, "Should get retreads for it."

Macias laughed. Patel saw Psych Techs Yee and Newsom approaching the front door and went over and opened the door to let them in. Yee came in first, and Patel said, "Good morning, Arlin."

Yee said, "Good morning."

Newsom came in next and said, "Good morning." Patel replied, "Morning," and closed the door.

The three walked toward the officer's station. Patel stopped at the first section, and the Psych techs continued to the last section. Bronson turned and walked toward the far end of the unit and heard familiar singing coming from cell 123.

"Bamba, bamba, la la la la bamba," Inmate Harris sang as he smiled at Bronson walking by.

"Hey, Ritchie," Bronson said. Harris's name wasn't Ritchie, but Bronson called him Ritchie because he was always singing the Ritchie Valens song. Bronson didn't know why, but Harris seemed to like him. He put on some rubber gloves from his glove pouch and continued toward the end of the unit to the cooler/cooker carts.

Macias yelled out to the unit, "Chow time."

Patel and Macias followed Bronson and joined up with the Psych techs at the carts. They rolled one cart to each side of the unit. As they got to each cell, one of them would unlock the narrow horizontal drop down door in the lower portion of the cell door. They would put a paper tray of food through the food port, along with a paper spoon and a carton of the beverage of the day. The inmate would take it, and the officer would close the food port.

Fortunately, the process to feed the thirty-three inmates didn't take as much time as some units with two hundred inmates. When they completed serving chow, the group rolled the empty carts back and wiped them down and put them by the back door.

They went back to the station and relaxed, talking and looking over paperwork for about twenty minutes. Newsom and Yee busied themselves reviewing medical reports. Bronson and his cohorts sat at the counter, looking at a computer or reading reports. Eventually, they became engaged in some light conversation. "Carl, are you going to bid out of this job?" Macias asked.

"No, I doubt the Warden's job is going to be open yet. I'll wait for a while," Patel said, smiling.

Macias nodded,. "Well, when you do decide to take over, make me you PIO."

Bronson chimed in, "When you guys make that move, warn me so I can transfer out of this joint to a camp far away from you."

"John, thought you had love for us," Macias stated. "Yeah, what's indicated here?" Patel added.

Bronson explained, "You guys would stick me in a first watch, sick relief job, with Monday and Thursdays off. That's the love you'd show me."

Macias offered to Bronson, "You could be my chief flunky. That would fit your skill set."

"Well, this flunky is gonna expand his skills and pick up the trash." Bronson paused. "You upper crust snobs can lower your station and help out." He picked up a large trash bag and shook it open. He headed over to cell 101.

"Trash out!" Bronson yelled loudly for the inmates. Macias said to Patel, "Did he say that to us?"

Patel said, "So much for love," and grabbed a trash bag, shook it open, and walked to the other side of the tier.

The crew busied their efforts opening the food port door and retrieving the empty trays and trash from each of the inmates and placing it in the trash bags. On completion of the task, they tied the bags and dropped them in a large bin at the back end of the unit. They returned to the officer's station. Macias picked up the 114 folder and sat down. "I'll do the 114s, even though it's a flunky's job."

Bronson chuffed, "Yeah, but don't draw any of those stick figure pictures in them again. The sarge gets upset."

Macias smiled. He proceeded to document on each inmates form that breakfast was fed and trash was collected. Bronson when over to a sink, took off his soiled gloves, and put them in the trash can. He washed his hands and put on a new pair of gloves. He walked over to cell 116 and began his tour of the inmate cells, taking note of the inmate and condition of the cell.

Some cells had a sign above it reading, "MAX," denoting maximum Ad Seg custody status. Because of over-crowding, some of the inmates were no longer on MAX status and yet remained in the unit.

As he came to MAX cell 123, he noticed that Inmate Harris was naked, sitting on his bed, holding his radio. "Ritchie. Dude, put some clothes on. You're scaring me."

Harris didn't respond. He only sat, swaying side to side.

Bronson stood and watched for a minute then continued his tour. He finished his rounds and came back to the officer's station. He got the attention of the Psych techs and his partners and said, "Harris is at it again. He's naked and quiet. That's not good."

Patel and Macias shook their heads. Bronson picked up the phone and said, "I'll call Sergeant Parks and let him know." He dialed the phone and waited for an answer.

"Sergeant Emery," was the response.

Bronson started, "Sergeant Emery, this is Bronson in Bravo 4 Bravo. Is Sergeant Parks there?"

"I'm covering for him today. What's up?"

Bronson continued, "Okay, I wanna give you a heads-up. Inmate Harris in 123 is sitting naked on his bed and not answering. He's a little 5150 and has a history of getting loud and assaultive when he starts out quiet and naked."

Emery paused and asked, "So he's stable for the moment?"

Bronson replied, "Yeah, and he sometimes settles down and puts his clothes back on. Letting you know just in case."

"Alright, let Psych know and keep me in the loop. I'll come by in a bit and check him out," Emery related.

"10-4, Sarge," Bronson replied and hung up. He started toward Harris's cell. Macias was there, talking to Harris, but Harris wasn't speaking. As Bronson got close, Harris seemed to notice him and started singing but not very loud. "La la la la bamba. La la la la bamba... bamba, bamba."

Bronson spoke, "Ritchie, what's going on?"

Harris mumbled something unintelligible and continued singing low for a few seconds, then he became quiet again. Yee came over and tried to get a response from Harris but to no avail.

Macias said, "Not much we can do except to keep an eye on him.

Patel came over and joined the conversation. Yee said, "I called the Chief Medical Officer and told her about Harris. She's checking his file and will call back."

"Well, I guess we should start a few non-MAX showers," Patel suggested.

Macias agreed. "Yep. Can't stop program unless something happens. Just have to keep an eye on him."

"Sergeant Emery is covering for Parks today, and he said he'd drop by in a little while," Bronson related.

"So either Harris will act up or settle down."

Patel turned and walked toward cell 116. Yee and Bronson went back to the officer's station. Macias stayed by Harris's cell, watching him for a minute or so and went back to the officer's station. Patel was at cell 116 and called into the non-MAX cell. "Nguyen, you wanna shower?"

Nguyen replied, "Yes, CO. Give me a minute."

Patel went over to a shower stall, unlocked it, stepped inside, and searched it for functioning and contraband. Satisfied, he left the door open and went back to Nguyen's cell.

Patel unlocked and opened the cell door and stood outside, waiting. Since Nguyen was not on MAX status, no restraints were required, only an escort. Nguyen came out, and Patel closed his cell door and locked it. He walked Nguyen down to the shower, and Nguyen went in. Patel closed the door and locked it.

Bronson was across the tier at 118, taking another inmate to a shower. Macias was at the officer's station on the computer. Patel joined Macias. Bronson locked his inmate in the shower and walked by Harris's cell and checked on him. There was no change in Harris, sitting quietly with the radio on his lap. Bronson walked back to the officer's station and stood, scanning the unit.

After about ten minutes, Inmate Nguyen called out to Patel, "CO Patel, I'm done."

Patel went around the counter and walked over to the shower. He unlocked it, and Nguyen came out. Patel escorted him to his cell. He unlocked the door and locked Nguyen back in. Patel went over to cell 110 and asked the inmate if he wanted a shower, and the inmate answered affirmatively.

Bronson stepped away from the counter and headed toward the shower to check on his inmate. As he passed by Harris's cell, he saw Harris standing bent over, putting something bloody in his mouth and gagging. There also was blood on his chest and more on his groin area. Bronson pressed his PAD alarm. He yelled out on the tier, "Code 3: cell 123 inmate down."

Macias sprung up from his chair. He looked over at Bronson, and as he responded to Bronson, he keyed his radio and advised, "Control, I have a Code 3 in Bravo 4 Bravo. Inmate down."

The radio emergency chatter continued. Patel, Macias, and Newsom got to the cell at about the same time. Macias exclaimed, "Holy shit."

Patel said, "What the hell!"

Bronson saw Yee at the counter and said, "Yee, bring us some masks and goggles."

Yee had started to respond to the cell but stopped and opened a cabinet, grabbed a handful of masks and some goggles, and sprinted to the scene. Bronson called to Harris, "Ritchie, whatcha doin'?"

Harris coughed something up. He reached down and picked up something and put it back in his mouth.

The crew already had gloves on, and they put on a surgical mask, but there were only two pair of goggles. The trio stepped into their PPEs and pulled them over their shoulders and zipped them up. Macias and Patel donned the goggles. Bronson said, "Okay. Gotta go in, okay?"

The pack agreed. Macias left to retrieve a shield. Harris backed toward the rear of the cell, grabbed his groin, and began squeezing it. More blood exuded from the pressure. Patel yelled, "Harris, stop!"

Patel opened the food port and drew out his OC pepper spray. Harris threw a towel over his head to shield an anticipated spray. Patel aimed surgically and spray a short burst of OC at Harris's groin. Harris yelled in pain from the pepper spray on the open wound in his groin.

The smell of OC permeated the air, masking the odor of sweat and blood. Harris dropped the towel to his groin and pushed on the towel and started to cough from the OC mist.

Macias returned with the shield. Two other officers were heard unlocking and entering the unit. Macias stood at the cell door. Bronson drew his baton and stood behind him. Patel readied his keys. Macias said, "Ready?"

Patel tapped Bronson on the shoulder; Bronson tapped Macias on the shoulder. Patel unlocked the cell door and swung it open. Macias rushed in toward Harris with the shield raised in front of him. Harris pulled his arms and shoulders together, bracing for impact. Bronson and Patel immediately followed Macias into the cell. As Macias made contact with the shield, Harris was squashed against the back of the cell from the weight of the three projectiles.

Harris moaned and continued to struggle to get free. Normally, a baton would be used to fend off any attack on the shield bearer, but no hand presented itself. Finally, Harris dropped to the floor and rolled on his stomach.

Macias coughed from the OC mist, saying, "Shield out," as he handed the shield back to Bronson while firmly putting his knee and shin on the shoulder and back of Harris and holding him down with his hands.

Bronson said, "Shield out," and handed the shield to Patel, who tossed it behind him on the floor.

Macias rotated to the left, keeping the pressure on Harris. Bronson put his baton away and retrieved his handcuffs and placed them on Harris. Bronson stifled a cough. "Cuffs on."

Macias eased off the pressure on Harris, and he and Bronson slowly lifted Harris to his feet and walked him out of the cell. Newsom had brought a gurney and blanket and placed it at the doorway of the cell. Bronson and Macias, with their eyes tearing, put Harris, moan-ing loudly, on the gurney. Bronson noticed Harris's testicle sack was torn open. Newsom covered Harris with the blanket.

Among the responding staff was Sergeant Emery. Emery keyed his radio, "Control, this is Bravo Sergeant Emery. I have a Code 4. No further assistance needed. One inmate en route to medical."

Radio traffic continued. The trio pulled down their masks to their neck areas and rolled the hoods back off their heads Bronson asked Harris, "Ritchie, why'd you do this?"

Harris responded, "I just wanted to die."

Sergeant Emery directed the responding officers to take Harris to medical. The officers nodded and rolled Harris out of the unit. Emery looked at the somewhat bloody group of combatants and asked, "Anybody hurt?"

They looked at each other and as a group shook their heads. Emery asked, "What happened?"

Bronson said, "We saw that he had blood on his groin. He was putting something bloody in his mouth and gagging."

Emery asked, "What was it?"

Bronson shook his head and turned and led the group back into the cell to see what was on the floor that Harris was eating. Bronson had to squint through tears as he looked closely and asked, "Is that—"

Macias finished the question: "Looks like a testicle."

They both had a scrunched up look on their face. "Ohhhhh," Bronson exclaimed.

Macias went over to the inmate's broken radio and picked up one of the several broken pieces and said, "I guess this is what he cut it with."

Bronson said, "Since it's not really a crime scene, I guess that's the only thing we would need to save." He paused. "Unless you want to save..." He looked at the chewed up testicle. They all turned and left the cell.

Emery came out shaking his head and coughing a bit. He said, "Okay, you guys should get cleaned up. I'll talk to you in a bit."

Macias said, "Okay. Thanks, Sarge."

The group peeled off to the bathroom to clean up and put on fresh PPE kits. Bronson was washing his hands when he remembered that he had left an inmate in a shower. He looked over at the shower and saw that the shower door was open and no inmate in sight. He walked directly across the tier to cell 118 and saw the inmate in his cell. "Who put you back in your cell?" Bronson asked.

"Yee put me back," he said. "Oh, okay," Bronson said.

Bronson saw Yee at the counter and walked over to him and said, "Thanks for putting my inmate in the shower away."

"That's okay. You were a little busy," Yee said. "Yeah. Thanks anyway."

Bronson went over to the end of the counters and sat down behind Patel and Macias. Bronson spun around on the chair and said, "Okay, guys, we having fun yet?"

He looked a Patel and stated, "Dude, you sprayed his groin? Really?"

Patel replied, "It took his mind off of our going in to extract him."

Bronson shook his head. Macias said, "Whatever works."

Patel paused a little and sang softly, "La la la bamba." Then he smiled and asked, "What's for lunch?"

They all chuckled. Bronson said, "Guess we have reports to write."

Macias said, "I'll wait till you do yours, and I'll copy and paste." Patel agreed, "Yeah, why should we all have to write a report?"

Bronson said, "I'll fix you guys. I'll wait until just before we get off, and you guys can stay late to copy and paste all you want."

They all laughed. Bronson spun back around and stood up. "Well, I gotta finish my last shower."

He went over to 101 and asked Ross if he wanted to shower.

Inmate Ross said, "Yeah."

Bronson went over to the shower and checked it for contraband. He came back to cell 101. Ross was standing at the door. Bronson opened the door, and Ross came out and headed toward the shower.

Bronson followed him and locked him in the shower. He went back to the counters and sat down at a computer. He opened up a file and started his incident report on Harris.

After a while, Inmate Ross called from the shower. "Hey, CO, I'm ready."

Bronson closed the screen on the computer and stood up. "Okay, Ross, on my way."

He walked over to the shower and opened the door. Ross started out the door but stopped and bent down to adjust a shower shoe. Bronson was behind him, watching him grab the shoe, when all of a sudden, Ross rose up quickly, swinging his right arm and fist at Bronson's face. Instinctively, Bronson partially blocked the blow with his right hand. Bronson grabbed Ross around his neck with his left arm, dropped his right arm down in between Ross's chest and right arm, hooked Ross's right elbow, twisted it and pinned it against Ross's back. Bronson rotated Ross to his left and, still holding him tightly, slammed him facedown on the floor with a thud.

Macias and Patel heard the noise from the shower door hitting the wall and Ross hitting the floor. They jumped up and ran to Bronson's aid. With their hands, knees, and elbows, they pounced on any available part of Ross's body, specifically his legs and head.

Bronson, still holding on to Ross's neck, grabbed Ross's hand and wrenched it behind Ross's back. Ross screamed with pain given by his subduers. Bronson moved his right leg onto Ross's right arm and retrieved his cuffs from his duty belt. He cuffed Ross's right wrist, slid his left arm from around Ross's neck, and cuffed the left wrist. Bronson said, "He's cuffed," and pressed his PAD alarm.

Macias yet had his knee on Ross's neck and shoulder. He stayed in that position for several seconds. Macias looked up at Bronson and said, "You sure? I think he's still fighting."

Patel, still leaning on Ross's back and legs with his knees, said, "Yeah, he feels like he's still fighting."

Ross was still moaning. After several more seconds, Patel and Macias left their positions and stood up. Responding staff stormed through the door into the unit. Sergeant Emery again was among the fray. He saw that they had Ross under control. Emery keyed his radio, "Control, this is Bravo sergeant, show a Code 4. No fur-

ther response needed. Staff assault and 10-15 in custody, en route to medical."

He had the responding staff take control of Ross. They rolled him to a sitting position with his back against the wall. Emery looked at the trio and asked, "Anyone hurt?"

He noticed a slight redness on Bronson's right cheekbone. "You, Bronson?"

"Not really. The guy spun on me getting out of the shower, and we had to take him down."

Emery looked at Ross. His face had several abrasions, and he had a bloody nose. He asked Ross, "Can you walk?"

Ross moaned and nodded. He turned to a couple of other officers and said, "Okay, guys, take him to medical."

The two officers stood Ross up. One of them said, "Whose cuffs? Bronson said, "Mine."

The officer turned Ross around and exchanged Bronson's cuffs for his cuffs and handed them back to Bronson. The same officer said, "Since this is our second trip here today, maybe we should come back and wait for another inmate to take to medical."

Bronson countered with a smile, "Maybe you could just take my place."

Emery broke into the discourse with his own smile. "Maybe I should just stick around too."

The officers escorted Ross out of the unit. Emery walked over to the officer's station with the three amigos. He leaned on the counter. "Bronson, you okay? You need medical, EAP, or time off, it's yours." Bronson shook his head. "Naw, Sarge, I'm good. He barely caught my cheek. I blocked most of the blow." He nodded at Patel and Macias. "These guys saved me."

They laughed. Macias said, "Hell, Ross was down, cuffed, and crying for his mama before we got out of our chairs."

They laughed again. Emery said, "Really, Bronson, what do you need?"

Bronson said, "Really, Sarge, I'm good."

"Okay, if you want someone to cover the rest of your shift, you got it."

Bronson said, "Only have a couple of hours left. I'm good."

"Well," he addressed all three officers, "I rolled in from the Bay two months ago, and it's been a change in operations for me. I'm adjusting to this joint, but it's good to see that there are good officers that have your back everywhere. You guys are first rate."

He shook each of their hands. He started to walk away but stopped. "Okay, but I'd like to know, who's taking the testicle for a souvenir?" He turned and left the building.

Patel went over and sat down at the computer. He sang softly, "La la la bamba."

Bronson smiled.

AND BABY MAKES THREE

Harmon eased up to the left side of the entrance road and pulled up into a parking space at Tower 8. He got out of his car, and as he walked to the base of the tower, he took a chit off of his key tag ring. A five-gallon plastic bucket was suspended on a rope coming out of the window in the top of the tower. He reached inside of the bucket, peeled off a single chit, and placed it in the bucket. The bucket was summarily hauled up to the open window in the tower.

Officer Geist leaned out the window, "Good morning, Harm." Harmon looked up at Geist. "Hey, Rob."

He heard the snap of the lock on the armory door in the bottom of the tower. He went to the door and opened it. He looked at the number on the key and matched it to the gun locker and unlocked the locker. He pulled off his holster and gun from his belt and placed it in the locker and locked it. He clipped the locker key on his duty belt. He left out of the armory door and closed it.

As he went back to his car, he yelled up to Geist, "Later, bud." He drove down the road to the parking lot and parked. He stepped out of his car, opened the rear door, took off his windbreaker, and put it in the car. He retrieved his lunch box from the back seat, closed the door, and locked it. He walked through the parking lot to the snack bar building. He opened the door and went inside. A CO and a couple of non-custody staff were sitting at a table. An inmate was wiping another table. Harmon stepped up to the counter, where Inmate Jones was waiting. Jones asked, "Can I help you, CO?"

"Sure," Harmon said. "How about a sausage sandwich?"

"Okay. Anything else?"

"That's it. Thank you," Harmon said. "Two-twenty," Jones said.

Harmon took out a script book from his shirt pocket and tore out 2.20 dollars in script and gave it to Jones. He put it into the till drawer and turned and went toward the back of the kitchen.

Harmon compared the clock on the wall with his watch. The clock was two minutes fast. Harmon saw Officer Parker step through the doorway of another dining room of the snack bar. Harmon extended his hand and fist bumped Parker's fist.

"You still working the back dock?" Harmon asked.

"Yeah, but I've got IST First Aid/CPR today," Parker replied. "You teaching it?"

"Not today. Working RC med yard on a swap."

"That's a good swap to take," Parker said.

"Yep, I thought so."

"Okay, guess I better get over there and play with the other dummies," Parker said.

"Okay, don't get confused who the REAL dummies are."

"Sometimes we wonder," Parker said.

Harmon patted Parker on his back as he left.

Inmate Jones caught Harmon's attention. "Order up, CO." Harmon went to the counter and picked up a paper sack con-

taining his sandwich and said, "Thanks, Jones."

Harmon put the sack in his lunch box and walked out the door. He crossed the circle drive and went into the Entrance Building. He walked to the counter and opened his lunch box for inspection and gave his ID to Officer Silva. "Good morning, Jack," she said.

"Mornin', Julie," he replied.

She looked into the lunch box and inspected his ID and handed it back to Harmon. "Almost time for your relief to show up," he stated.

"Yeah, pretty much that time," she replied.

Harmon put his ID away and picked up his lunch box and walked toward the sally port door. The lock on the door popped, and he stepped into the sally port. He nodded to the officer in Tower 1. The gate slid open, and he walked through and walked across an interior roadway and into the administration building and continued through the building into a courtyard that ended at a large steel door. He stood at the door, looked up at a camera, and yelled, "South door."

Momentarily, the lock on the door snapped, and he opened it and stepped into a short sally port and closed the door. The lock on the heavy iron grill gate in front of him snapped, and he pushed it open, walked through, and closed it. He turned left and headed down a long corridor with two orange stripes painted in the center. Automatically, he took the center route that ostensibly was used for staff and the outside meant for inmates.

Several doors were spaced on either side of the length of the corridor. He walked past doors to L-Wing, classification, the infirmary and took note of a refrigerated drinking fountain that staff rarely drank from, probably due to the suspicious taste of the water.

Continuing down the corridor, Harmon saw West Corridor Officer Evans standing by the K Wing (Ad Seg) door. As he approached Evans, he put out his hand for a high five. Evans accommodated the gesture and said, "Harm, baby, what's up?"

Harmon paused momentarily and replied, "You tell me. You da man."

They exchanged wide smiles, and Harmon continued past C, D, and E wing doors on the left and H and J wings on the right.

As he got to the RC (Reception Center) Grill gate, he looked into the F and G Wing units, searching for any unit staff nearby. No one was close enough to greet, so he continued through the grill gate and past the canteen area. He arrived at the East Hall unit door and looked in. Officer Wong was at a desk in the Officers' area. He noticed Harmon at the door and got up. Wong went over to the grill gate that separated them, unlocked it, and opened it. He extended his hand, and Harmon took it.

"Jack, buddy, how's it going?"

"Just working my tail off, as usual," Harmon said.

"Yeah, you forget who you are talking to?" Wong said with a grin.

"Yes, I do. The biggest dump truck at DVI," Harmon retorted with an equal grin.

Wong let go of the handshake, and they slapped it to a quick low-five handshake. Harmon looked down the tier and then up above to the unit control panel above. "Is Clark here today?"

"She's over in R&R. A bus came in," Wong stated.

Harmon nodded. "Okay, gotta go work in the salt mine. No rest for the weary."

"To hear you tell it, sure," Wong stated.

Harmon smiled and shook his head and said, "Okay. Later, you top slacker, you."

Harmon turned and walked across the hallway to RC Control. He took off his chit key ring from his belt and separated six chits and put them in the control room window. He sat his lunch box on the floor. Officer Medina was at a desk. She stood up and went to the window and picked up the chits. "Morning, Harmon. What you got?"

"Med corridor," Harmon replied. "I'm Williams today."

"Gotcha," she replied.

She turned and began collecting equipment from around the room, replacing each piece with a chit. She came back to the window and placed the equipment on the window shelf. "Here you go," she said with a partial smile.

"Thanks, Medina."

Harmon put each piece of equipment in its place on his duty belt: cuffs, baton, radio, OC spray, and two groups of keys. He picked up his lunch box and looked at the clock on the wall in the control room. He went around the corner and walked down the corridor toward receiving and release (R&R). As he approached the R&R door, he unclipped a group of keys, selected one big key, unlocked the door, stepped in, and locked it behind him. At the holding cells on the right,

Officer Clark was standing outside one of the holding cells, looking at a sheet of paper and talking to some inmates. He saw Harmon coming in. "What's your name and number?" she asked one of the inmates.

"Dombarangian, AA-56382," was the reply.

Looking at another inmate, she asked, "How about you, sir?

Your name and number?"

"Powell, AA-10222," was the answer.

Harmon patted Clark on the shoulder as he went by. Clark nodded to Harmon and said, "Hey, Harm, what's up?"

"See you got some intake for East Hall," Harmon stated. "Yep, got five more guests."

"Job security in process," Harmon offered. "Sadly, that's the case."

"Well, I'll let you guys get acquainted," Harmon said. "Thanks, buddy," Clark said with a smirk.

Harmon walked past the holding cells and the package room on the left then around to the right toward the R&R office. Sergeant Hall was sitting at the counter, perusing the stacks of intake files. Officer Almenderas was standing next to the sergeant, sorting a stack of papers. Harmon continued down the hallway, where the R&R crew was gathered outside a room of about twenty of the new inmate arrivals off of the transportation bus. Harmon greeted Officer Pierce with handshake and Yee with a fist bump. Yee said, "Jack, just in time. Transportation Officer Upton here has a test for us."

Harmon went up to Upton and shook his hand and asked, "Okay, what's the test?"

Upton began, "I was apprising your cohorts that, among this fine selection of incarcerants, is a perpetrator of various sections of the penal code of the 288 variety. And I behoove you, as indomitable correctional elite, to ascertain the identity of said individual, harnessing your vast experience and intuition in that endeavor."

Harmon laughed and said, "I can see why I'm just in time because I'd say Pierce and Yee have no idea what you are asking." Harmon looked at Yee and Pierce with a big smirk.

Yee said, "Thanks for the insult."

Harmon continued, "However, I'll break it down for them. You want us to pick out the child molester."

"These two think they know which one it is," Upton stated.

Harmon paused and said, "Well, let me see if I can match wits with these two Hoggs."

He gazed around the room, sizing up the usual suspects. He noted the age, ethnicity, physical stature, and where they were in the room relative to the other inmates. He focused in on three candidates that had little interaction with the others and seemed to be seated purposefully somewhat by themselves. He turned to Upton and said, "Since I don't see any facial injuries, I assume that the other inmates don't know his crime."

Upton said, "That would be my guess. The PVSP staff told us about him on the down-low."

Harmon again scanned all of the suspects, looking at the condition of their attire and their group interactions. He kept coming back to the original three. He intentionally caught the eye of each of them. All had a look of uncertainty and/or fear about them. He turned to his buddies and said, "I got three possibilities. And unless that young dude next to the right corner has a good poker-face, I'll take the older white gent next to the gate here."

Pierce laughed and said, "You and me, homie. That's my choice." Yee said, "I picked the one you passed on."

Pierce looked at Upton. "What say you?"

Upton paused and turned one corner of his lip up. He looked at Pierce and Harmon and finally declared, "Okay, you two are right." Pierce and Harmon gave each other a high five. Yee shook his head in disappointment. Pierce said to Harmon, "We still got it,

huh?"

Harmon smiled and shook Upton's hand. "Thanks for the fun time."

"Always my pleasure," he replied.

Harmon turned and went back to the R&R office and walked over to Almenderas and asked, "You ready to disseminate the newbies to the units?"

Almenderas picked up several 154s and said, "Take your pick and give Yee the others."

"Thanks, Gordy."

Harmon turned and went out of the office and called out, "Yee, baby, you've got mail," waving the inmate movement slips.

"Oh, Yaaaaay," Yee said as he walked toward Harmon. Harmon separated the slips and held them up in two hands.

"You want to take F and G wings, and I'll take West Hall?" Yee nodded and said, "That's cool."

Harmon handed one bunch to Yee. Harmon and Yee went back to the room to the new intakes. Yee read from the slips and called out names and numbers. One by one, the inmates were taken out of the room and lined up in the hallway. Yee directed them to follow him out of R&R.

Harmon did the same with his group of inmates, who followed him out of R&R. Harmon had the inmates stop when they exited the unit and had them line up against the wall to the right. He spoke to the group. "Gentlemen, welcome to DVI. I'm Officer Harmon. You can call officers 'CO' if you wish. We are not deputies. You have reservations in West Hall. When you are walking, you will walk in single file to the right side of the hallway with your hands behind your back, and try to refrain from talking. For your safety, do not stop in front of a doorway. If there are parallel lines painted on the center of the floor, unless directed otherwise by staff, you will not walk in the center. That is for staff. Walk to the right."

Harmon continued, "If there is loud buzzing sound, that is an alarm. There may also be flashing lights. If you are walking stop and stand against the right side of the wall, do not come off of the wall. That will be deemed an aggressive act, and you may suffer consequences. There may be a red light in a hallway. You will stop where you are until the light goes out. If there is an alarm and you are standing in a chow hall, move against the wall or if you are seated. Remain seated with feet under the table. If you are in a yard or open area and there is an alarm, you will have a seat on the ground. Custody staff will direct you as to what to do. Carry your ID with you at all times and surrender it when requested."

Harmon paused scanned the group and asked, "Are there any questions?"

There were a few shaking of heads and a smattering of "No" and "No, sir" answers.

Harmon continued, "Okay, thank you for your attention.

Follow me." He began walking.

As they got close to the T intersection, he said, "Make a left, guys."

The group did as instructed. When they got to the West Hall door, he had them stop. He stepped into the doorway of the unit and saw Officer Carter in the unit. Carter saw Harmon and unlocked the grill gate. Harmon spoke. "Got some intake for you, Carter."

"Okay, bring 'em in."

Harmon stepped back out of the unit and said, "Okay, guys, West Hall awaits."

He swept his hand into the unit. The inmates filed in, and Carter had them stop inside. Harmon gave Carter the 154 slips and said, "I told them about alarms and movement during alarms."

"Thanks, Harm," Carter said. He walked over to the dining hall door and unlocked it. He ushered the inmates inside and had them sit at the tables.

Harmon asked, "You all good, Carter?"

"Yeah. Thanks, Harm."

"Can I leave my lunch in your officer's station?

"Sure. I might get hungry later," Carter said, grinning.

Harmon turned and went to the officer's station and put his lunch box in a corner of the station and exited the unit, closing the grill gate behind him. In front of this unit is a large 120-foot-by-60- foot chain-link fenced-in yard. The yard is tucked into two sides of an L shaped RC Medical building with a walkway if front of each part of the building.

Harmon went to the right and noticed an inmate waiting at the gate near one end of the L shaped building. Harmon approached the inmate and asked, "What are you waiting for?"

The inmate said, "I'm Hawley, the RC Med orderly." Harmon nodded and asked, "Where you live?"

"J-233 upper."

"You have you ID and assignment card?"

"Yes, sir CO," Hawley said and promptly produced his ID and assignment card.

Harmon took a long look at the documents. "How long you worked this job?" Harmon inquired.

"Almost a year," he replied.

"What's your crime, and how much time you get?"

"Selling. Two years. I'm short to the house. Three months left."

"Selling meth?"

"No, leaf."

"Must have been a lot of weed to get two years. What county?"

"Humboldt."

"Wow," Harmon said, shaking his head. He gave Hawley back his cards. "Okay, let's pat you down, guy."

Hawley seemed surprised at the request but immediately complied by facing away and putting his arms out to his sides. Harmon did a thorough pat down of Hawley. He inspected the sack lunch he was holding in his hand for contraband. When he finished, he unlocked the gate, and they both went inside.

Hawley went over to a locker on the walkway and got out a couple of towels and a spray bottle and began wiping windows and sills.

Harmon went into the dental office and saw two women busy at work. Dr. Bonett was wearing a white medical smock. She was sorting some dental tools that the other woman was disinfecting. "Good morning. I'm Harmon. I'm your 'Officer Williams' for the day."

Dr. Bonett looked up at Harmon and came to him with her hand extended. Harmon shook her hand and she said, "I'm Dr. Bonett. I remember you from last year when you worked for Williams during his vacation."

Harmon nodded. "That's right. Hope it was a pleasant memory."

"Of course," she said, smiling, and she motioned to the other notably younger woman. "And this is my dental technician, Moore." Moore half smiled at Harmon and said, "Good morning, officer."

Harmon replied, "Morning. I've seen you in the hallways, but it's good to get your name to match with your face." Harmon paused. "You can call me Harm or Harmon, if you'd like."

He continued, "You ladies ready for the onslaught?" Dr. Bonett replied, "When they come, we'll be ready."

"Sounds good. I'll put them in the yard until you call for 'em."

"Okay, thank you," Bonett said.

Harmon turned and went out the door. He went to the right and walked down the walkway, stopping at the Psychologist's office door, which was locked. He retrieved a key group from his belt and unlocked the door. He went inside and scanned the room and each cubicle within. Satisfied that nothing was out of sorts, he went back out and locked the door.

He continued around to the right side of the L shaped building to the Physical Therapy unit. He opened the door and saw Therapists Bagley and Nguyen at their desks. Inmate Hawley was dry-mopping the floor. Harmon went over to Bagley and said, "Good morning."

Bagley nodded. "Morning, Harmon. Need me to straighten out your back?"

He put his hands together, making two fists and snapping them downward in a breaking motion. Harmon laughed and said, "You'd like to do that."

Nguyen heard Bagley's comment and chimed in, "Whatever he doesn't fix, I will."

Nguyen stomped his heel into the floor and made grinding motion with his heel. Harmon shook his head and laughed as he walked away saying, "You know, you guys should be a tag team in the WWF. I'm outa here."

Harmon left the office and continued down the walkway and checked the remaining two offices. Next, Harmon unlocked the gate to the yard and walked around the interior perimeter of the yard and then walked a grid pattern, looking for anything suspicious in the grass or dirt. Any disturbed area can reveal hidden treasures, weapons, drugs, metal pieces, or money. After he finished, he posted up at one of the gates to the yard.

Harmon's job for the day was to check in the inmates that were issued a ducket or a pass to receive the services in this complex. When the housing unit gives an inmate a pass, he comes to the gate, and the officer checks the pass for date, time, and service needed and checks the inmates ID. Then the inmate is put in the grassy yard to wait to be called. When he is called, the officer escorts him to the office. When he finishes, the officer escorts him out to the hallway, and the inmate would return to his housing unit. It's a continuous process, and inmates often try to finagle their way into places they shouldn't be or hang out and delay their return back to their cell.

Occasionally, an inmate tries to make a hookup for some sort of contraband—drugs, weapons—or to pass notes. The officer has the responsibility to prevent or discover such activities by searching and being aware of inmate activities.

The day for Harmon was, so far, normal for this job. There were a few slackers and attempts to go to a different office.

Harmon also was cognizant of the activities of his orderly Hawley. An orderly is a prime resource or target for nefarious activities. They have access to all sorts of contraband in offices and also can mule contraband. It was a relief that in his observance of Hawley, he was meticulous in his cleaning and engaged very little with the other inmates. He kept busy, often sweeping and cleaning an area several times in a routine. He appeared to be a good worker.

Harmon searched Hawley's work locker several times during the shift, checking his sack lunch, clothing, and the locker itself. He pulled the locker away from the wall, checked the back of the locker, then he put the locker and its back and checked the bottom.

The day was winding down, only two inmates left on the yard. Shortly, Bagley stepped out of his office and signaled me that he was ready for the last two inmates to go to Physical Therapy. Harmon was on the opposite side of the yard in front of West Hall under the overhang. He unlocked a gate and went into the yard and locked it. He waved at the last two inmates to meet him at the other gate. They all arrived at the gate at the same time. Harmon opened the gate and let the inmates in to the walkway and pointed to Bagley, waiting at the door.

As he locked the gate, he saw Dr. Bonett walking toward him past the inmate bathroom. Hawley was cleaning the inmate bathroom; he had placed the mop bucket in the doorway. Harmon followed the inmates to Bagley and ushered the inmates inside. Bagley said, "Guess these are it for the day."

"Want me to go rustle up some more clients?" Harmon quipped.

Bagley chuckled, "No, thanks. We're good," and went back inside the room.

Bonett was walking past Harmon, and he joined her. "Tough day?" he asked.

"Not really. Just another day," she replied. "Miss Moore still in the office?" Harmon asked. "No, she left a little bit ago," Bonett stated.

Harmon looked quizzically and said, "Really? I didn't see her go by."

"Oh, she usually waits in Psych, Therapy, or the clinic for one of her friends, and they walk out together," Bonett offered.

As they got to the gate at the end of the hallway, Bonett had her staff key in her hand and unlocked the gate. She and Harmon went through, and Harmon locked the gate. He walked with her around to the left and continued to RC control. Harmon said, "Okay, Doc. It was good to see you again."

She nodded. "Yes it was nice to see you too."

"Be safe, Doc," he said as he continued on to the left hallway. Harmon had a little break in the action and went into West Hall to his lunch box and got out a bottle of water and his half-eaten sandwich, leaving the lunch box there. He went back out and stood next to the wall in the shade under the overhang. He began to eat the sandwich. He finished the sandwich and his bottle of water and went into the unit and tossed the remnants into the trash in the office.

He went back outside and walked back around the yard fence past RC control to the gate he and Dr. Bonett came out of. He went up to the Psych office; the door was locked. Harmon unlocked it and went in. He walked around the room, looking for any occupants. He saw a copier had been left on, and he turned it off. He saw no one and went back out and locked the door. He walked a little farther and unlocked the door to the clinic and performed the same search for occupants.

Finding none, he went over to the Physical Therapy office and went inside. He saw Nguyen exercising the arm of an inmate. They nodded at each other. He walked around to the right and saw Bagley watching an inmate on a step machine. Harmon checked the remaining areas and saw no one else. He went back to Nguyen and asked, "Did Ms. Moore from dental come by?"

"Didn't see her today, but she likes to walk out with us or someone in the other offices." he explained.

Harmon was curious. "Hmm...there's no one in the clinic or Psych, and Dr. Bonett said she left earlier." Harmon's anxiety increased. He somewhat quickly exited the office. He stepped lively over to the inmate bathroom, where the mop bucket was yet in the doorway. He pushed the bucket aside and entered the room. Since there are no enclosures in the bathroom, only two open toilets; it was obvious that no one was there. *Where is Hawley?* he thought.

Scanning the area for Hawley, Harmon quickly walked over to the dental office. He turned the doorknob, and it was locked. He quickly unlocked the door and hastily searched the rooms. He heard some noises in the last room and stepped in. Hawley saw Harmon, and Hawley practically froze in position with his pants down as Ms. Moore struggled to cover herself.

Harmon was both relieved and somewhat amused at his discovery. He tried to keep an eye on Hawley while avoiding seeing Ms. Moore. "Hawley, pull you pants up," Harmon ordered.

"Ms. Moore, are you hurt?" Harmon asked. Moore ashamedly and softly answered, "No."

Hawley finished pulling up his pants. "Okay, Hawley, sit in that chair and don't move," Harmon directed.

Harmon leaned into his shoulder where his radio mic was clipped. He paused, searching for what to say. Finally, he found some words. He keyed the mic. "RC sergeant, Harmon."

The radio responded. "Go for, Sergeant Hall."

"Sarge, I need assistance in the RC dental office. Can you and an S&E, 10-19 ASAP. 10-15 in custody. Code 4."

"Okay, Hawley, stand up and turn around," Harmon said as he took his cuffs off his belt. He handcuffed Hawley and searched his pant area, took him by the arm, led him a few steps out of the room, and said, "Sit on the floor and don't move."

The radio crackled. "Harmon, Sergeant Hall. Is this a 10-33?" Harmon tried to explain, "Sarge, I have an inmate in custody.

It's Code 4, but I need you to 10-19 RC dental with and S&E."

"10-4 Harmon, en route," was the reply.

Moore finished gathering herself and sat in a chair with a few tears rolling down her cheeks. She asked, "What you want me to do?"

Harmon thought for a second. "Ms. Moore, I suggest you just sit there and don't say anything to anyone."

About a minute had passed when Harmon heard the door to the office open. A voice called out, "Harmon, where are you?"

Harmon responded, "Here in the back."

Sergeant Hall and Officer Medeiros came into view. Sergeant Hall saw Hawley sitting handcuffed on the floor. He couldn't see Ms. Moore. "What you got, Harm?' Hall asked.

Harmon half grinned, took half a breath, and said, "Medeiros, can you take inmate Hawley to a holding cell?"

Medeiros tentatively said, "Sure."

"Did he assault you?" Hall asked.

Harmon squinted, shook his head, and said, "No." Hall got impatient. "Okay, then what?"

Harmon paused and said, "Well...it may be a case of friendly persuasion assault."

Hall said, "What the hell does that mean? Friendly persuasion assault?"

Harmon stepped back away from the entrance to the room and showed Hall Ms. Moore sitting in the chair. Hall was surprised and intrigued and worried. He asked Moore, "Are you hurt, Ms.?"

Moore said, "No, I'm not hurt."

Harmon explained. "I couldn't find clarity my orderly, Hawley. I was also concerned that I didn't see Ms. Moore leave. So...I eventually found them here together and otherwise engaged, so to speak."

Finally, the pieces came together for Hall. Perplexed, Hall paused and said slowly and deliberately, "Okay!"

Harmon sat in his recliner, sort of watching TV and drinking iced tea. His phone rang with a familiar ring tone. He reached over and answered. "Hey, Bill. What's up, buddy?"

"Hey, Jack. What's going on? Haven't talked to you for a couple of weeks."

"Yeah, took some time off. The woman and I decided to take a drive up the coast. Went to the redwoods and hit a couple of beaches."

"How's SCC treating you? I miss working together."

"Yeah, me too, but the drive to DVI was too long."

"I hear that. A twenty-minute drive beats an hour and a half anytime."

Harmon thought for a moment. "Hey, how about you and Susie meet us for dinner at Olive Garden Friday?"

"Sounds good. I'll check her schedule and let you know."

"Great." Harmon paused. "Hey, Bill, you still working 3 yard?"

"Yep. Still lovin' it."

Harmon continued, "You know a couple of weeks ago, I was working a swap in RC med yard, and I rolled upon an inmate and non-custody female dental tech in the dental office. He was filling her cavity."

Bill chuckled. "You're kidding. Really?"

Harmon asserted the truth. "No, shit, but," he continued, "that's only part of the story. When they rolled him up, they found a couple of sonograms of the baby that she sent him."

"Must have been a long term relationship."

"Yeah, but here's the kicker. They transferred him to your joint, and I heard he is on the 3 Yard," Harmon added.

Bill was intrigued. "What's the guy's name?"

"Hawley," Harmon answered.

Bill laughed. "That dude is in my unit."

"Nooooo," Harmon said incredulously. "Yeah. He's in 114 or something," Bill stated.

The two exchanged stories for about an hour and ended their call with plans to meet.

*****

Bill was recalling his unit from chow, monitoring the inmates coming back. He was closing doors on the first tier. He went over to close the door on Hawley's cell. He looked in at Hawley and paused and said to Hawley, "Hawley, seen any sonograms lately?"

Hawley was taken by surprise. "What?"

As Bill closed the cell door, he sang a tune, "Just Molly and me, and baby makes three."

CONSEQUENCES (NOT SO SHOCKING)

Metal Fabrication Instructor Paris went into the warehouse office. Receiving Clerk Myers was sitting at her desk. She saw Paris, nodded to him, and said, Good morning, Shelby."

"Good morning, Maggie. Here to pick up my order," Paris replied.

Myers shuffled through a few papers and selected one page. "Here it is." She read from the invoice, "Two cases of bolts and nuts, fifteen six-foot straps, twenty eight-gauge sheets, two boxes of welding rods, 6011 and 7018, and a case of red spray paint." She handed him the invoice.

Paris scanned the invoice. "Yep, looks good."

"It's at B dock," she stated.

"Thanks, Maggie," he said, smiling. He turned and left the office.

He walked past several dock bays and out of the warehouse. He went over to the state vehicle, a one-ton dually truck, and unlocked the door. He fired it up and drove around the warehouse to B dock bay and backed up close to the dock. He got out of the truck and went to the rear and dropped the tailgate all the way down, then got back in the truck and backed it up to the dock. He got out of the truck, taking his keys and clipping them to his belt. He went up the steps into the warehouse and walked over to the pallet of materials. He checked the load to ensure it was secure.

He walked over and jumped on a forklift, put the seatbelt on, and started it up. He raised and lowered and tilted the blades back and forth. He backed up, stopped, then pulled forward and stopped. Satisfied, the lift was operational. He spun the forklift around and slid the blades into the pallet and lifted it up a few inches off the floor. He carefully guided the pallet of material onto the bed of the truck and dropped it in place. He parked the forklift back into its space. He went out and got into the truck and left the warehouse area.

He drove around to the rear of the institution to the vehicle sally port. He stepped out of the vehicle and looked up at Officer Hughes in the gun tower.

Hughes saw Paris get out of the vehicle and pressed a button on the panel in the tower and spoke, "Paris at your gate."

Officer Wagner, in the office in the vehicle sally port below Tower 7, pressed a button and said, "Thanks, Hughes. Let him in."

Hughes activated the gate entrance switch, and the enormous gate began to slide open. Paris got back into his truck, and when the gate was completely open, he drove into the sally port straddling his vehicle over a three-foot-wide pit. As the gate started to close, Paris popped the hood open and stepped out of the truck.

Wagner's partner, Officer Hernandez, walked into the pit and inspected the under-carriage of the vehicle and came back top-side. Wagner checked under the hood, inside the cab of the vehicle, and the bed of the truck. Paris gave Wagner his ID. Wagner looked at the ID, smiled, and said, "Shelby, you need to get a better picture on your ID. This one is flat-ass ugly."

Paris shook his head and said, "I'm so sorry, Al. You were looking at the mirror I put over my picture."

Wagner laughed and handed back the ID. Hernandez overheard the conversation and said, "You guys practicing your stand-up routine again?"

Wagner said, "I would, but I'd need a straight man to do the other part, but Shelby is anything but straight."

Paris smiled and countered, "You didn't complain last night, baby."

Wagner and Paris laughed, hand-grabbed and man-hugged, then fist bumped. Paris said, "Okay, let me out of here. I've got places to go."

Wagner yelled up to Hughes in the tower, "Open big north!"

As the gate slid open, Paris got back in his truck and waited for the gate to finish its journey then drove through.

*****

Paris drove up to the metal fabrication gate, got out of the truck, unlocked the gate and opened it, drove through, then closed and locked it. He backed up to the metal shop and stopped, took the truck keys, and clipped them to his belt. While Inmates Phillips, Chow, and Brown busied themselves unloading the truck, Paris went to his office, unlocked the door, and went in and sat down at his desk.

*****

Looking through the glass floor above the sally port, C-3 Control Officer Seagle was watching the inmates exiting his unit out to the exercise yard. Officer Beaber was on the floor of the unit, checking inmate IDs as they exited. Officer Colson was on the second tier, watching the inmates on the opposite side of the unit exit their cells on the second tier and go down the stairs.

When the last of the inmates had exited the unit, Seagle went to the control panel and closed the doors on each end of the sally port. She watched her officers as they secured the unit. Beaber went over to each of the cells on the first tier and checked for occupants and slid each cell door close as he went. Colson went over to the cells on the second tier and did the same on the second tier.

When all the doors were closed, Seagle went over to the yard observation window and stood for a while, watching the yard. Beaber went into the officer's station and sat down at a desk and filled in the Daily Activity Report log.

Colson was still on the tier and went over to cell 232 and called out to Seagle, "Seagle, open 232."

Seagle turned from the yard window and went to the control panel and opened cell door 232. "Doing a cell search," Colson stated. He went into the cell.

Seagle's face scrunched somewhat. She went over to the floor above the officer's station and opened up a small glass door in the floor to talk to Beaber. "Pete, Colson is searching 232 again," she said.

Beaber looked up at Seagle and took an intentional breath. He closed the logbook. "Wonder what he's up to now?"

"Probably no good," Seagle said.

"Guess I better check it out," Beaber said with a sigh. Beaber started to get up when the phone rang.

Colson went over to the bottom bunk and pulled the sheets and blanket off of the mattress and tossed them on the floor. He pulled the mattress off and tossed it on the floor. He stood on the bedding and mattress and pulled the bedding and mattress off of the top bunk onto the floor. He reached under the lower bunk and pulled out a box and dumped it on the floor. He saw some photos that were in the box, took them, crumpled them up, and went over to the desk and took some papers off the desk and put the papers and photos in a paper bag used for trash. He saw some family photos on the wall and tore several off the wall and tore them in half and tossed them on the desk. He turned and went back out of the cell and closed the door.

Seagle saw Colson come out of the cell. Beaber finished the phone call and stood up. Seagle softly spoke to Beaber, "He's out of the cell now. He was only in there for less than a minute."

"Well, doesn't mean he wasn't up to something. I'll go check it out," Beaber said.

Seagle said, "You might want to wait a while before you see what's up."

"Screw that. He makes it tough on all of us," Beaber exhorted. "Don't let the workers out of their cells yet."

Seagle said, "Gotcha."

After Colson left the cell, he walked around the rest of the second tier, went down the stairs, and sat at one of the tables in the dayroom with his back to cell 232.

Inmates Rice and Parker in cell 201, with a view directly across from cell 232, had been watching Colson in the cell. Rice said, "Aaron, that piece of shit looks like he's at it again."

Parker replied, "That's fucked up. He's an asshole. He's always screwing with someone."

Rice commented, "But he trashed Ruben's cell again."

Beaber began his trek out of the office and started up the stairs to the second tier. Rice saw him and yelled out the edge of his door to Beaber, "Hey, Beaber, did you see what that CO did? Check out 232."

Beaber, without looking over at Rice's cell, held up a hand in a stop signal and continued up the stairs. Seagle was watching Beaber, as were Rice and Parker. Beaber stopped in front of 232 and looked in the narrow window. He saw the bedding in the floor of the cell. He shook his head and held up his hand above the cell door and called out, "232!"

Seagle pressed a button on the panel, and the door slid open. Colson heard Beaber call out and turned and looked up at 232 and stood up. He mumbled to himself and started toward the stairs. Beaber went into the cell and began picking up the blankets and sheets and started to fold them up. Momentarily, Colson showed up in the doorway. "Pete, whatcha doing? I just searched this cell," Colson stated.

Beaber turned to Colson, shook his head, and said, "Colson, you're an ass. What's your problem? You can't just trash a cell like this and call it a cell search."

"That's the way I found it," Colson said.

"You F'n shittin' me. This is a Southern cell. They don't leave their house like this. That's not allowed," Beaber stated.

"That's the way I found it!" Colson insisted.

Beaber took a breath and stared at Colson and said, "Just take your ass off the tier."

Colson stared back for a moment. He turned and walked back down the tier. Beaber put the mattresses back on the bunks and finished folding the bedding and blankets somewhat decently and placed them on the mattresses. He picked up the contents that were in the dumped box and put them back in the box. He saw the torn photos on the desk and placed them back together as best he could. He scanned the rest of the cell and stepped back out. "Close 232," he called out. He went down the stairs and back to the officer's station.

*****

Inmate Phillips knocked on the door of Paris's office. Paris got up from his chair and opened the door. Phillips said, "Boss, I rotated the welding rods and put the new boxes behind the old ones."

Paris nodded. "Thanks, Phillips. How's that cage fabrication going?"

Phillips replied, "Looks good so far. Brown had to fix my welding screwup, though. He's such a perfectionist. He ground some weld off and rewelded it. Guess it wasn't pretty enough."

"That's why he gets the big bucks," Paris said, laughing. Phillips chuckled. "Yeah, what, ten cents more an hour?"

"Well, he was the top welder for NASA until he messed up,"
Paris added.

"I'm learning a lot from him," Phillips said.

"Me too," Paris stated. "You guys better take your lunch break.
I gotta go to plant ops." Phillips nodded and left.

Paris went out of his office and locked the door. He walked over to the metal-fab gate, unlocked it, and opened it. He got in the truck, pulled it out the gate, got out of the truck, and closed and locked the gate. He climbed back into the truck and drove off.

*****

Seagle was looking out of the yard window, waiting for the hourly unit unlock for inmates to return to their cells or go out to the yard. She looked at the clock and went over to the small glass door to the office in the floor of the control unit. She asked Beaber if he was ready for the unlock. Beaber nodded and went out of the office, locked the door behind him, and stood on the floor in the center of the unit. Colson was waiting for the inmate movement at the inside gate.

Seagle pushed the buttons that slid open the inside and outside sally port doors. Colson went through the sally port and stood outside the unit, checking IDs of inmates returning. Seagle went over to the main unit panel and watched for inmates to use a fly swat to stick out of the edges of their cell door and wave it against the wall to let the control officer know they wanted out. The inmates in 201 used their fly swat, and the door opened. Parker and Rice went down the stairs and left the unit along with several other inmates.

On the yard, Rice saw Inmate Martin playing handball on the Southern handball court. Rice walked over to the handball court and stood well away from the court so as not to invade the Southern's perimeter. He stood for a while and got the attention of Martin with a heads-up nod. Martin walked over to Rice. "What's up?" Martin asked.

Rice nodded. "Just a little 411 for you. Colson searched your house, and it looked like a trash job."

Martin's face grew sour.

Rice continued, "Beaber went up to your house, and him 'n Colson had some words. Seems like Beaber was pissed, and Colson split."

"Okay, thanks, dude." Martin nodded.

Rice left, and Martin walked over to his cellmate Baron. "Hey, homie, we gotta get back to the house. That *puta* Colson might be fuckin' with us. He searched our house again."

Baron nodded. "Tenemos que atrapar el siguiente desbloqueo." Martin agreed. "Si, we gotta catch the next unlock."

The two grabbed hands in solidarity.

*****

Hughes looked out of his tower along the dual fence line with the electrified fence dead center between them. The towers are generally spaced one hundred yards plus along the fence line. Except for the vehicle or pedestrian entrance towers, the perimeter towers are not normally physically manned, except during maintenance. The actual type of wire and voltage are not generally shared with the public. However, it is universally accepted that it is a formidable deterrent to its breach along with the razor wire-topped double chain link fence.

Activation and deactivation of the electrified fence are a slow intricate procedure and requires specially trained staff. Thus far, no one, except birds and small animals, has tested its merits. There is a low-amperage rodent wire at the base of the fence to ward off critters. Additionally, random patrols and often pressure sensors are added features to prevent intrusion.

*****

Seagle finished her lunch and was wandering around the control booth that has a 180-degree view of the housing unit and of two tiers of fifty cells each. She heard Beaber call her name. She went over to the glass porthole in the floor and asked Beaber, "What's up?"

"Ready for the unlock?" Beaber asked.

Seagle looked at her watch and said, "Wow, yeah, guess it is time."

Beaber stepped out of the office and waited for Colson. Seagle went back over to the main control panel and opened the interior sally port gate. Colson went through the sally port and waited for the outside door to open. When the door opened, Colson went out and stood by the door, monitoring the inmates coming in.

Martin and Baron were among the first to enter the unit and stood by their cell door. Seagle methodically opened each cell door for the inmates standing by their doors. Martin and Baron went into their cell and noticed their bedding was on their mattresses. That was normal for a cell search, but Baron immediately noticed the torn pictures on the desk. "Chingad chingada estupido," he emoted.

Martin checked other parts of the cell and noticed the box under the bed had been gone through. Eventually, he checked the trash bag and found the papers and photos that Colson had thrown into the trash. Martin and Baron talked softly to each other, but their faces showed anger. They spent the next hour in meaningful deliberation. The last unlock came none too soon for the two soldados.

Martin collected a fly swat and waved it out of the space between the cell door and the wall. Soon, their door opened, and they hurried down the stairs toward the opened sally port doors. Beaber motioned Martin over to him and said, "Martin, I want to talk to you two about your cell."

Martin acted nonchalant and said, "It's all good, CO. No problem."

Beaber was taken aback by Martin's lack of concern. "Can we go now?" Martin asked.

Beaber looked at Martin and Baron suspiciously. "Yeah, okay," he surrendered.

The two scurried out of the housing unit and headed toward the Sureno section of the yard. They went over to Inmate Mendoza, the shot caller on the yard, and made their case. Colson had animosity toward Latino inmates. He had a history of physically assaulting Hispanics and claiming he had been assaulted. He had planted contraband, including weapons, on inmates and in their cells. He had written up inmates for being out of bounds after he had lured them to that location. This latest action against Martin and Baron was one of a long list of trashing of cells and destroying property.

Several inmate appeals and charges of disparate treatment had either been denied or reduced. Mendoza listened to Martin and Baron's accounts, along with several other aggrieved inmates. Mendoza thought for a moment and said, "Esperate, voy a hablar con Agurrie." He turned and walked toward the Norteno basketball court.

He approached the sentry standing guard by the basketball court and asked to talk to his boss. The inmate left Mendoza and went over to Aguirre and told him Mendoza wanted to talk to him. Aguirre nodded and walked over to Mendoza.

It's usually a matter of respect among rivals to meet to discuss an action that affects both of their factions. Mendoza was sanctioning a hit on Colson and was giving Aguirre a heads-up since all Hispanics may suffer the consequences. Aguirre seemed to understand the reasons for the hit, as his soldados had been victimized also.

Mendoza returned back from the conference and went to his lieutenant on the yard. He turned and went over to Martin and Baron and nodded. In short course, several of the inmates left and reappeared. They surreptitiously talked two at a time and transferred items among them. It was getting close to shift change, and about ten of the group split into groups of two and lay in wait at each outside corner of Building 3.

Yard Officer Olsen had been standing near the Indian sweat lodge, watching the yard and took note that the two shot callers had spoken to each other. That was not always a good sign. After they separated, he watched for a minute and went over to a phone box on the wall and unlocked it. He dialed the number to the yard gun. Officer Beltran manned the C yard gun, which was a room of sorts attached to the wall thirty feet above the yard on the building across from the housing units. There is a full view of the entire yard and heavy glass door openings on the floor for viewing or discharging a weapon. The phone rang, "Beltran, C yard gun," was the response. "Robbie, Olsen. Just saw Mendoza and Aguirre in a pow-wow on the Norteno basketball court."

Beltran picked up his binoculars and focused in on Aguirre and then Mendoza. "What you think, buddy?"

"Not sure, but there was some activity by the Suerenos," Olson related.

"You think they're trying to solve a problem?" Beltran asked. "Again, not sure, but I'm gonna let the sergeant know," Olson stated.

Beltran said, "10-4," and hung up. He began closely scanning the yard.

Seagle was leaning down, talking to Beaber through the floor opening when she heard a voice on a speaker. "Three, control."

She stood up and went over to the yard window and saw Officer Riley at the entrance below. She opened the outside door. Riley stepped in and waited at a door just inside the sally port. The outside door closed, and the lock on the first door popped, and Riley stepped into a small room with a second door directly in front of him—in effect, a mini sally port. He closed the first door behind him, and the second door lock popped, and he went through, closed it, and went up a flight of stairs. Seagle went over to the main panel. Riley sat his lunch container on a table in the center of the control room. "Busy day?" he said to Seagle.

Seagle responded, "Fairly normal."

She went closer to Riley and spoke softly, "Colson trashed another cell, 232."

Riley shook his head and said, "Again? When's that guy ever gonna learn. He's had several 602 inmate appeals filed on him."

Seagle replied, "We know he hates Mexicans, but he doesn't listen. It'll catch up to him sooner or later."

Riley nodded and said, "Probably so."

Riley turned and busied himself checking inventory in the control room. He walked by the floor port above the office, and Beaber caught Riley's attention. "Did Kim tell you about Colson?"

Riley nodded, pursing his lips as an acknowledgment.

When Riley finished the inventory, he went over to Seagle and said, "Okay, Kim, you're good to go."

A voice from the outside sally port door called out, "Three, staff on your door."

Riley told Seagle, "Head on down, and I'll let them in."

Seagle picked up her jacket and lunch box and went down the stairs. The door popped open, and Seagle stepped through into the mini sally port and waited. The outside door on the sally port entrance slid open, and Officers Nevis and Silva entered, and the door slid closed. Riley opened the first door off of the mini sally port and let Seagle into the main sally port. Seagle nodded to Nevis and Silva. "Afternoon guys."

Nevis responded, "Hey, Kim," and Silva nodded.

The inside gate slip open, and they all went into the unit. Beaber was in the officer's station, finishing some paperwork. He had heard the door open and stepped out to meet the trio. Beaber yelled out to Colson seated at a table in the dayroom, "Colson, our relief is here." Nevis and Silva put their lunch containers in the office and came back out. Nevis went over to where Colson was sitting. Colson removed his duty equipment—keys, radio, cuffs, spray, baton, and alarm—and handed them to Nevis. Beaber and Silva went back into the office, and

Beaber gave his duty equipment to Silva. "Anything going on?" Silva asked.

Beaber's face wrinkled and spoke quietly, "Colson. I'll let Riley fill you in."

Silva lifted his eyebrows and delivered a drawn out "Okay."

"We all good?" Beaber asked Silva.

"Yep, all good," Silva responded.

Beaber stepped out of the office and called to Colson. "Colson, you coming?"

Colson turned from Nevis, said nothing, and walked into the sally port. Seagle and Beaber looked at each other and shrugged off the non-answer. They picked up their lunch boxes and followed Colson into the sally port. From above, Riley watched them enter the sally port, then closed the inside gate. The outer door slid open, and Colson walked quickly onto the yard ahead of Beaber and Seagle. Seagle said, "Guess he's in a hurry."

Colson took a shortcut from the cement walkway and went across the dirt around the corner of the housing unit. On the opposite corner of the building, two pairs of inmates saw Colson exit the building and walked very quickly to intercept Colson as he rounded the corner of the unit. They were trying not to run as that would bring attention to them.

Beaber and Seagle were talking as they walked. They both noticed the inmates were almost running. Seagle and Beaber both yelled to the inmates, "Hey, slow down. Walk."

The inmates disregarded the orders. Beaber and Seagle quickened their pace also. As Colson had rounded the corner of the build-

ing, the other inmates that were waiting on that side ran up behind Colson and pushed him to the ground and began kicking and hitting him. The other group of inmates caught up to the frenzy. Among the assailants were Martin and Baron. Their blows were delivered with sharpened metal weapons.

Beaber and Seagle arrived at the melee within seconds. "Get down!"

"Stop," "Yard down!" were shouts coming from the two.

Seagle kicked one of the inmates, and both she and Beaber swung their lunch boxes and hit any attacker within range. Inmates on the yard, hearing the shouts to get down, gradually began to comply.

Yard Gun Beltran used his yard PA to echo the orders. He had picked up his Mini-14 and was trying to decide if he needed to shoot or not. He racked a round into the chamber that echoed on the yard. That action caused most of the inmates close by to stop and lay down. Officer Olson appeared out of nowhere, spraying the attacking inmates. Beaber and Seagle were pushing and kicking inmates away from Colson. The attacking inmates didn't seem to be interested in other staff, just Colson.

Beltran saw inmates attacking an officer but didn't see any weapons, although it appeared the motions used were stabbing or slashing motions. He didn't have a clear shot, given staff was involved in the incident. Beltran leveled his rifle aim at a large open patch on the ground and discharged one round. The inmates on the yard all lay down. The attackers at the Building 3 area scampered away from the incident, tossing any weapons away. Other officers from the yard and housing units swarmed the area.

Colson was lying on his side and sat up. He had blood coming from a wound on his right arm. Colson was trying to stand up, and Beaber went over to help him stand up. Seagle helped responding staff restrain and identify attackers. Beaber helped Colson walk out of the area.

*****

Paris waved to Central Services Officer Austin driving by as Paris arrived at the metal-fab gate. Paris got out of his truck, opened the metal-fab gate, and drove in through the gate. Paris was getting back out of his truck to close the gate when he heard the gunshot from C yard. He paused for a moment. He went over to his office, leaving his truck running and the door open. He ran to his office, unlocked the door to the office, and picked up the radio off of his desk. He hurried back toward the truck.

Inmate Chow saw the door to the truck open. He ran to the truck, jumped in, and closed the door. He backed the truck out of the fabrication yard and turned it around.

Paris saw his truck leaving the yard gate. He ran to lock the metal fab gate. He keyed up his radio. "Officer Austin, Paris."

Officer Austin was driving on a service cart on the central access road that split the center of the institution between two pairs of yards: A and B, and C and D.

"Go for, Austin," he responded.

"10-19 metal fab gate ASAP. Need some help with an inmate," Paris urged.

Austin was headed in the right direction toward metal-fab. "10- 4, en route." He stepped down on the accelerator of the electric cart.

Chow sped off toward the vehicle sally port. He veered to the right and took direct aim at the fence just to the left of Tower 5.

In Tower 7, above the vehicle sally port, Hughes saw the truck speeding out of the plant ops area. He called down to Wagner and Hernandez. "Hey, Paris is driving like hell down the side road."

Wagner hurried over to the gate to get a better look. Gaining as much speed as possible, Chow rammed into the interior fence, and the truck bottomed out on the cement footing of the deadly electrified fence. The truck was stuck.

Both Hughes and Wagner saw the truck plow into the fence near Tower 5. "Holy shit, what's Paris doing?" Hughes exclaimed.

Hughes got on the radio. "OP, Tower 7, 10-19 Tower 5 perimeter ASAP. There's a truck stuck in the electrified fence."

Officer Miller, the Outside Patrol (OP), was on the perimeter road near Tower 4 when he heard this most unexpected call ever. "Tower 7, there's what in the fence?" Miller asked.

"There's a truck on the fence. It drove through from the inside road," Hughes restated.

"OP copies. En route."

Now, Watch Commander Chamberlain, a seasoned veteran of twenty-four years and six institutions, had been monitoring the radio traffic, as was his duty. However, the incident happening on C yard seemed enough for his plate, but NO—this call stunned him for a moment. He waited for the exchange between the OP and Tower 7 to finish. He thought for a moment and keyed his mic. "Break, this is the Watch Commander. Any unit in the vicinity of the truck on the fence, please advise."

Officer Austin was listening to the radio traffic and neared the metal-fab gate but didn't see Paris at the metal fab gate. Austin replied to the Watch Commander, "This is Austin. I'm one away from Tower 5."

"Watch 1 copies."

Austin and Miller arrived at the scene at the same time. Austin stopped his cart and jumped off and ran over to the back of the truck, careful not to touch anything. He didn't see any electrical arcing.

In between the fences was an improbable sight with dangerous implications. The truck was just as Officer Hughes had said, partly through the interior fence and impaled on the electrified portion of the fences.

Inmate Chow was dazed and had been tossed into the passenger side of the truck. He sat there for a couple of minutes. The air bags were wrapped partially around his legs.

Austin saw inmate Chow stirring in the truck. He shouted at Chow, "You in the truck, don't move. You can get shocked. Are you okay?" He knew it was a stupid question but it was already out of his mouth. "What's your name?"

Chow was gathering his thoughts and finally answered, "Okay."

"Are you okay? What's your name?" Austin repeated.

Chow sat up in the truck seat, and Austin recognized him. He wondered where Paris was. "Chow, are you okay?" Austin asked.

Chow replied, "Yeah, okay." Austin added, "Is Paris with you?" Chow replied, "No."

Austin was relieved and somewhat confused. He wondered where Paris was. "Stay there. Don't move. Don't touch ANYTHING," he emphasized.

Chow said, "Okay, I'll stay here."

Austin thought to himself, *That's a good choice.*

Miller was at the outside fence near Tower 5. He had his hand on his gun but didn't draw his weapon. He reasoned that if the inmate tried to escape, he'd have to survive the electrical current and climb the twelve-foot fence topped with razor wire. He just stood there and watched.

Two officers came running up to where Austin was, and the OP Sergeant drove up to accompany Miller on the outside fence. Austin keyed his radio. "Watch 1. Austin."

"Go for Watch 1, Austin."

"We have a Code 4. No further response is necessary. We have four officers and the OP Sergeant on scene," he reported. "The truck is stuck on the electrified fence. An inmate was driving the truck. The inmate says he's okay for now. I advised him to stay where he is and not to move."

"Watch 1 copies."

Chamberlain stepped out of his office and looked at his Watch Sergeant with a half grin on his face. He took a breath. "As soon as we can, man Towers 4, 5, and 6 and get a team down to deactivate that section of the fence, so we can get the inmate to safety."

The Watch Sergeant nodded, "Got it, Lieu."

Chamberlain went back into his office and sat down at his desk. He said to himself, "An inmate was driving. What the hell.? He dialed the Warden's number.

As the afternoon dragged on to evening, the two major incidents were eventually controlled. The Warden called the Director, who, in turn, called the Governor about the electrified fence breach. Inmate Chow was extracted without being shocked to death, and the yard assault was cleared. Colson suffered stab wounds and cuts, but there was nothing life threatening. The investigations revealed that staff's ill-advised actions have consequences, while some inmate actions are not so shocking.

ABOUT THE AUTHOR

Terol McCullar spent his first forty-two years working dozens of jobs, gaining life experience, preparing for a career that brought him personal satisfaction as a California Correctional Officer and Sergeant Instructor known as T-Mac.

The author has acquired an insight into the passions and obstacles that form the basis for one's self-motivation. His own motivation has been molded, having lived through the changes witnessed from the 1950s and 1960s to the present. The dichotomy of witnessing both good times and turmoil was tempered by the belief in self-efficacy. The author's passion for the law and teaching is commingled with his being a Singer/Songwriter.

The author acknowledges the undying support of his wife Tricia, daughter Angela, and a long list of great friends.